THE PERKS OF BEING A PARKER

KAY CORRELL

ZURA LU PUBLISHING, LLC

Published by Zura Lu Publishing LLC

Over thirty years. That's how long we've been checking in with each other every single morning. I so appreciate your constant support and encouragement on this writing journey of ours.

Thank you, Kat, Margery, Michelle, and Vicki.

ABOUT THIS BOOK

Livy and Austin finally get their wedding. Or do they?

Charlie, Livy's father, shows up after years and years of being a no-show in her life and starts causing problems. And who does he connect with? **Camille!** And, what a surprise, Camille is stirring up trouble, yet again.

Cassandra is back in town for the wedding and might finally have that date with Delbert. If it actually happens this time. Oh, and there's a charity ball *and* a fire at Cabot Hotel. Are you ready for the exciting conclusion to the Moonbeam Bay series?*

*(Not saying there will never be another book in this series, because, as you know, Kay

can never just leave her characters behind.) But we can all be assured these characters will pop up in other series, just like they always do.

Be sure to look for the next series, Blue Heron Cottages.

KAY'S BOOKS

Find more information on all my books at
kaycorrell.com

COMFORT CROSSING ~ THE SERIES

The Shop on Main - Book One
The Memory Box - Book Two
The Christmas Cottage - A Holiday Novella
(Book 2.5)
The Letter - Book Three
The Christmas Scarf - A Holiday Novella
(Book 3.5)
The Magnolia Cafe - Book Four
The Unexpected Wedding - Book Five

The Wedding in the Grove - (a crossover short

story between series - with Josephine and Paul from The Letter.)

LIGHTHOUSE POINT ~ THE SERIES
Wish Upon a Shell - Book One
Wedding on the Beach - Book Two
Love at the Lighthouse - Book Three
Cottage near the Point - Book Four
Return to the Island - Book Five
Bungalow by the Bay - Book Six

CHARMING INN ~ Return to Lighthouse Point
One Simple Wish - Book One
Two of a Kind - Book Two
Three Little Things - Book Three
Four Short Weeks - Book Four
Five Years or So - Book Five
Six Hours Away - Book Six
Charming Christmas - Book Seven

SWEET RIVER ~ THE SERIES
A Dream to Believe in - Book One
A Memory to Cherish - Book Two
A Song to Remember - Book Three
A Time to Forgive - Book Four
A Summer of Secrets - Book Five

A Moment in the Moonlight - Book Six

MOONBEAM BAY ~ THE SERIES
The Parker Women - Book One
The Parker Cafe - Book Two
A Heather Parker Original - Book Three
The Parker Family Secret - Book Four
Grace Parker's Peach Pie - Book Five
The Perks of Being a Parker - Book Six

BLUE HERON COTTAGES ~ THE SERIES
A six-book series coming in 2022.

WIND CHIME BEACH ~ A stand-alone novel

INDIGO BAY ~ A multi-author sweet romance series

Sweet Days by the Bay - Kay's Complete Collection of stories in the Indigo Bay series

Sign up for my newsletter at my website *kaycorrell.com* to make sure you don't miss any new releases or sales.

CHAPTER 1

Olivia sat with Austin at the edge of the beach at Blue Heron Cottages, checking her watch time and again in between scooping up handfuls of sand and letting it slip through her fingers. Neither did anything to make the time go any faster.

Austin chuckled. "They'll be here when they get here. My sister texted when they arrived at the airport, and then they had to rent two cars to haul everyone here. I'm sure they'll be here soon."

She jumped up from the beach chairs tucked under the palms in the shade. "I'm a little nervous about meeting your family." Actually, she was really nervous. So many people to meet. Would they like her? Think that she was a good fit for Austin? In addition to Austin's parents, his two brothers, two sisters, one brother-in-law, and two nieces were also coming for the wedding.

Austin stood and tugged playfully at her arm. "I can take your mind off worrying about meeting my family."

"Really? How's that?"

"Guess what? It's only four days until we get married, you know." He sent her a boyish, teasing grin.

She rolled her eyes. "I'm well aware of that, but I'm not sure that helps my stress level."

"Anyway, I wanted my family to come in a bit early so Mom could rest up." He pressed a kiss to her cheek. "I'm forever grateful you moved up the wedding so Mom could be here."

She leaned against him and wrapped her arms around his waist. "Of course. I know how much it means to you to have her here."

"It does."

"And it means a lot to me, too."

"Let's go walk up to the cottages. They should be here soon. Can't wait to see them." They held hands and headed toward the cottages to wait for his family's arrival.

Soon two minivans pulled up. The doors

slid open and people started tumbling out. Two men who looked a lot like Austin but with lighter hair. Two women laughing and helping a pair of red-haired twins out of their car seats.

The two girls squealed with delight and hit the ground running. "Uncle Austin!" They raced to him, reaching up, putting their sticky hands on his clean shirt.

He scooped them up, seeming not to care. "How are my little princesses today?"

"Uncle Austin, we're not really princesses you know," one of the girls said, a serious expression on her round little face.

"Really?" Austin's eyes widened, and he winked. "I was sure you were."

One of his sisters helped their mother across the drive. Her eyes looked tired, and her body was frail, clothes hanging slightly large on her frame. Austin said she'd lost a lot of weight. She had short wisps of gray hair, but not a lot of it. A welcoming smile lit her face as she crossed the drive holding onto her daughter's arm, a bit unsteady on her feet.

Mrs. Woods held out her hand and grasped Olivia's. "Livy, dear, I'm so glad to meet the woman who has made my son so happy."

She clasped the woman's hands in hers. "I'm so glad to meet you, Mrs. Woods."

"Oh, you must call me Genevieve."

Austin's father walked up, clapped his son on his back, and turned to her. "And I'm Wilson. Great to finally meet you." The man had to be at least six foot four and towered over his wife as he stood beside her.

"It's great to meet you, too."

"These are my sisters, Trina and Terry." Austin leaned over and let the twins down. Trina is the mother of these two cuties. And that's her husband, Nick." Austin smiled down at the girls who clung to his legs. "And my brothers, Bob and Dan."

One of the little girls looked up at her. "And I'm Ashley, and she's Abby. I'm bigger."

How in the world was she going to keep all this straight? She tried to repeat each name in her mind and put a face with the name.

Violet, the owner of the cottages, came out to greet them. "You must be the Woods family. I'm so happy to have you as my very first guests."

"The place looks charming," Genevieve said as she glanced around the colorful cottages.

"I hope everything goes smoothly. Kind of a test run for my grand opening next week. I'm glad I was able to have Livy's and Austin's wedding here."

"How about we get checked into our cottages and let Momma have a bit of a rest?" Wilson took Genevieve's arm, concern hovering in his eyes, not quite disguised by his broad smile.

"I am a bit tired from the traveling."

"You and Mr. Woods are going to be in the teal cottage. You could head on in there if you want. The door is unlocked, key is on the counter."

"I think I'll do that."

"I'll get everyone checked in. How about that?" Terry offered. "That means Trina can wrangle the twins, and my strong, strapping brothers can handle the luggage."

Genevieve turned to her. "I really am so pleased to be here for your wedding. We must find time to sit and talk and get to know each other a bit better."

"Why don't you rest now? And I'll make sure to make time to have a nice long visit with you." Olivia nodded to the woman.

"I'd like that." Genevieve held onto Wilson's

arm and they slowly headed toward the teal cottage.

"The trip really tired her, but she'll perk up after a nap," Trina said as she headed off to capture the twins who were headed in the direction of the beach. "No, girls. Not yet. We need to unpack. Then I'll take you to the beach."

The family dispersed in different directions, and Austin turned to her. "And that, my love, is my family. Now you've met them all. That wasn't so bad, was it?"

She grinned. "Nah, but I hope I call everyone by the right name."

"If you mess up with the twins, they'll be sure to correct you." He winked at her. "Come on. We're supposed to meet Heather at Sea Glass Cafe. She's got some last-minute wedding stuff to go over with us."

They headed off to the cafe while she repeated the names in her head. *Was it Trina or Terry who had the twins?* And she was positive she didn't know which brother was Bob and which was Dan. Was Bob the taller of the two? She didn't want to admit her confusion to Austin and ask him, but she was going to have to sort this all out quickly.

Cassandra Cabot could hardly contain her excitement. Part of the reason was Livy's wedding this weekend. She was still getting used to her newfound family after her uncle found out he had a grown daughter—Donna, Livy's mom. But she had to admit, part of it was getting to stay at The Cabot Hotel again…

… and getting to see Delbert Hamilton, the new owner.

The car pulled up the wide driveway that flowed in a sweeping arc in front of the hotel. A smile came to her lips, and her heart leapt at the familiarity of the scene. The Cabot, even though her family hadn't owned it for years, was still the only place that truly felt like home to her.

The driver got out, opened her door, and retrieved her luggage from the trunk. She thanked him and started up the stairs to the front door.

"Cassandra, there you are." Delbert hurried down the steps toward her, a wide, enthusiastic smile spreading across his features.

Her heart pounded at the sight of him,

which was silly, of course. A grown woman shouldn't feel like a schoolgirl with a crush.

And yet... she did.

"I'm so glad you're finally here." He kissed her lightly and quickly on the cheek. The kind of kiss a friend would give to another friend. Was that how he considered her? They'd scheduled a date months ago, but she was called out of town on business and it never happened. Maybe this time they'd make good on the raincheck.

"I know, it's been a while since I've been back to Moonbeam. I've been so busy at work. But I did take some extra time off so I can stay a bit after the wedding. I miss seeing Uncle Ted. And, of course, there's my new family." And time to spend with Delbert, but she didn't say that out loud.

His brown eyes twinkled with warmth, and she tried not to stare at him. He was dressed in gray pants with a crisp crease down each leg and a light blue button-down shirt with faint, narrow stripes to it. His tie was perfectly coordinated to his outfit. He always dressed the part of a businessman, even in the more casual atmosphere of Moonbeam.

And he was so very handsome. Very. She couldn't ignore that.

"Here, I'll take your luggage. I reserved the Bay Suite for you." He reached for the handle of her large suitcase with one hand and took her elbow with his other, leading her inside.

The lobby of the newly refurbished hotel took her breath away. Sparkling, welcoming, and ever so familiar. Like the hotel was opening its arms to her, welcoming her home. She let out a long sigh. "I love this hotel."

"And she's glad to have you here again." Delbert led her to the elevator—that was nicely remodeled with wooden walls and fresh carpeting—and they rode to the top floor.

At the Bay Suite, Del opened the door for her. She stepped inside and instantly felt like she was home. No matter where she'd lived since her family had closed the hotel, no house, no place, had felt like home. Not like this. "Del, thank you for reserving this suite for me."

"I know it's your favorite."

"It is. And it still looks just like it did when I was a young girl." She walked over and looked out the French doors toward the sea. "I love this view."

He left her luggage near the door and came to stand beside her. "So, I was wondering. I know you're here for Livy's wedding and to see your uncle, but will you have time to go to dinner with me while you're here? I thought maybe I could take you up on that raincheck. We could have the dinner we had to cancel last time?"

"Yes, I'll absolutely have time. I'd love to." Her heart skittered in her chest again. Maybe they would finally have that date. The date she'd wanted with Delbert Hamilton for over thirty years. Nothing was going to stop her this time. Not work. Not anything.

"Tomorrow night?"

"Oh, tomorrow Donna is having the family over to get to know Austin's family better. Then there is the rehearsal the next evening and then the wedding."

"Then Sunday night? Would that work?"

"That would work. I'll look forward to it." Her heart skipped again in anticipation.

"And could I escort you to the wedding?"

"I was going to go with Uncle Ted and Patricia, but it probably would be easier to go with you. Save them a trip of coming over here to pick me up." Easier? Had she just said it was *easier?*

Not that she'd *love* to go with him.

That it was a *great* idea.

That she'd look *forward* to it.

No, she'd said it was easier…

"Fine. I'll pick you up here at your room at five?"

"That would be nice. Thank you." So polite. So formal. What was wrong with her?

"I should leave you to get unpacked then." He gave her a small smile and left.

She pulled the suitcase to the adjoining bedroom and threw herself on the bed, a wide grin spreading across her face. First, she'd go to the wedding with Del, then they'd have their first official date. So far this trip was shaping up to be a wonderful visit.

CHAPTER 2

Del whistled under his breath as he left Cassandra's room, elated at all the time he'd be able to spend with her. He would reserve the private dining room at the Cabot for their dinner on Sunday. Just like he'd done for their first ill-fated attempt at a date.

Meal choices filtered through his mind, and he decided he'd have the chef make up his delicious red snapper dish with asparagus on the side. He also made a wonderful salad with fresh strawberries and walnuts with a light vinaigrette dressing. And a nice bottle of wine, of course. And he'd order in some flowers. He wanted the night to be perfect and hoped his luck would hold and nothing would cause them to cancel again.

As a bonus, he'd be escorting her to Livy and Austin's wedding. He couldn't be more pleased. He wanted all the time he could possibly get with Cassandra while she was in town this trip. Rarely was he this captivated with a woman.

Oh, he'd dated Camille for a long time. Years, actually. But Camille, while she could be charming when she wanted to be, was just a lot of work. Relief had overcome him when he broke up with her months ago. He saw her now and again, most often on some rich CEO's arm. And she regularly came to eat at The Cabot— which he couldn't really stop her from doing, but he'd like to. There were a million other places to eat at in the area. Some much fancier and much more to her expensive taste than The Cabot.

But, unfortunately, she kept showing up. Especially when they hosted any event that she thought would be attended by *important* people. People she wanted to get to know.

Or maybe she wanted to flaunt her string of new men in front of him. But didn't she realize that he just did *not* care? She could date who she wanted... only preferably far, far from his hotel.

They did have a large fundraiser dinner

scheduled for the ballroom this coming week. It was sure to attract many of the state's movers and shakers. State senators and representatives. The mayors of Moonbeam and Belle Island were coming. The CEO of the largest regional bank was invited. He wouldn't be surprised if Camille showed up with one of them. He shook his head as he headed toward the dining room to talk to the manager and then the chef to make arrangements for his dinner with Cassandra.

He'd worry about Camille later. Or maybe he could ignore her. But he'd promised to make an appearance at the fundraiser, and Camille was always a loose cannon. You never knew what she might say. He'd thought he might ask Cassandra to go with him to the event, but now that he thought about it, he wasn't so sure.

But then, it was silly to let Camille have any control over his life at this stage. Fine, he'd ask Cassandra if she wanted to come with him. The fundraiser was for the Moonbeam Bay History Museum. The museum was bringing over some of their items for display. Cassandra was sure to be interested in that.

With that decided, he headed off to make preparations for his date.

~

Cassandra met her uncle and Patricia at Portside Grill out on the wharf. Ted rose from his seat at the table and gave her a hug. "Cassie, so good to see you. I've missed you."

She hugged him back, welcoming the familiarity of his arms. "I've missed you. I'm sorry I've been away so long." She turned to Patricia. "Good to see you, too."

"Your uncle has been quite excited about your visit." Patricia gave her a polite smile.

She'd only met Patricia a few times, and the woman was still a bit standoffish with her. According to Livy, Patricia was fairly—how had she put it—opinionated and a bit critical, but had relaxed a bit since dating Ted.

Cassandra wondered if Ted and Patricia were getting serious. They'd been dating awhile, and her uncle had asked if she'd mind if Patricia joined them tonight. Of course, she didn't mind, especially in the spirit of getting to know Patricia better. Or letting Patricia get to know her better. This woman who had captured her uncle's attention years ago, and now once again. Not to mention the mother of his daughter, even if she had kept it a secret from him for all those years. It all seemed to have worked out in the end.

They ordered their meals, and Ted chose a bottle of wine to accompany their dinners. He always seemed to know the perfect wine, and she was glad to go with his suggestion.

"So, Cassie, how is work going?" Ted poured her a glass of wine and handed it to her.

"It's going great. I'm about ready to close on a deal for another group foster home. It's in a perfect location. Good school district and right across from a park. It would house six kids and I already have a wonderful couple who would run it. That's what has been keeping me so busy."

"That sounds great. I'm glad you can find these smaller living situations for these kids."

"The fundraising for them is almost a full-time job in and of itself. But I love my work." She turned to Patricia. "And how are things going for the wedding?"

"The last I talked to Donna, she said Olivia had everything in place. And you're going to Donna's tomorrow to meet Austin's family, aren't you? Ted and I will be there."

"I am. I'm looking forward to meeting his family." And getting to know her new family better, too. "I was sorry to miss Heather's wedding. But it was the night of a big fundraiser I was hosting, or I would have been here for it, for sure."

"It was lovely. They had it on Jesse's boat out in the harbor. At sunset." Patricia gave a delicate shrug of her shoulder. "I wasn't really sure about her having it on a boat, but it did turn out to be a lovely choice."

"When I last talked to Livy, she said that having her wedding at Blue Heron Cottages was your idea."

Patricia's lips curved into a small smile. "I surprised myself with that suggestion. I'm not really one for outdoor weddings, but when Olivia moved up the date and was having such a hard time finding a venue, the idea just kind of popped into my head. They do have a lovely courtyard at the cottages where the wedding will be. And this way Austin's family can stay there at the cottages. It worked out quite nicely."

"And I heard that Violet and her brother, Rob, are officially opening the cottages up the next week? Having their grand opening?"

"I believe so. You heard that Rob and my daughter Evelyn are dating, right? He seems like a nice man. An author. I've never met an actual author before meeting him."

"I did hear that. I'm looking forward to getting to know him." Who knew when her uncle found out he had a grown daughter that she'd end up with such a large extended family?

Their meals came, and she glanced furtively at her uncle as they ate, watching the way he looked at Patricia. There was a definite connection between them. If she got some time alone with him, she was going to ask him how things were going. He looked totally smitten with Patricia, and if her hunch was right, Patricia was pretty fond of Ted, too. They had this way of glancing at each other or smiling at each other. An intimate connection, as if no one else was around.

And it suited her just fine if they were serious. She'd love for her uncle to find someone. He was such a great guy and his happiness meant everything to her.

They finished their meal and walked along the wharf. The twinkle lights strung above them tossed a magical light along the walkway. The wharf was one of her favorite places in Moonbeam. Well, after The Cabot Hotel.

They strolled along until they got to the end of the wharf. "Thanks for dinner, Uncle Ted. It was nice catching up with you. And, Patricia, nice to see you again."

"It was nice seeing you. We'll see you tomorrow night at Donna's." Patricia's hand rested on Ted's arm, and he covered it with his own.

She hid a small smile. Yes, there was definitely something going on there.

"Good night. Glad you made it back to town." Ted nodded then led Patricia out to the parking lot. She watched them leave, arm in arm. Her uncle looked so happy tonight. And she thought she might have made a tiny bit of headway with getting Patricia to like her. Or at least get to know her.

All in all, a pretty nice night. She turned and headed off to The Cabot.

CHAPTER 3

Donna looked around the lanai, making sure everything was ready for the party for Austin's family. She was so glad her daughter had found Austin. They seemed like the perfect match. Double bonus that Emily adored him. The three of them would be a perfect family.

Her husband, Barry, came outside carting a cooler of beer, sodas, and water. "All iced up." He gave her that smile of his. The one that shouldn't make her go all weak in the knees at her age, but it did. Even after months of marriage. He looked so handsome in shorts and a Hawaiian print shirt. He'd really adapted to life down here in Florida.

She was lucky to have found him. So far her family was doing wonderfully in the luck department. She and Barry married, Livy and Austin were getting married, Heather and Jesse had just gotten married. Oh, and Evelyn was dating Rob Bentley, whose sister Violet ran the Blue Heron Cottages. She loved it when things seemed to come together for her family.

Barry set the cooler at the edge of the lanai and came over and pressed a kiss to her cheek. "It all looks great."

"Thank you." She'd put out lanterns around the edge of the lanai that should pop on as it darkened at sunset. She had a stack of extra resin Adirondack chairs she kept for large gatherings such as this that she'd scattered around in groups so people could sit and chat.

"Evelyn just got here. She popped the seafood shell casseroles in the oven. Said she'd be out in a few minutes. She brought some peach pies, too."

"Of course, she did. I told her I made brownies, but you know Evelyn. She loves to cook. Besides, everyone loves her peach pie." She leaned against Barry, and he wrapped an arm around her waist. Besides adoring the man, she loved how comfortable he was to be with and how supportive he was of her. She'd worried they'd have a bit of an adjustment when he moved in after the wedding. They'd both lived alone for so long. But it really hadn't taken long to find a new rhythm to their married life.

Evelyn stepped outside. "It looks lovely, Donna. The peonies are beautiful."

"I couldn't resist getting some for a few arrangements. They were so pretty in the different shades of pink."

"Hi, Mom. The place looks great." Olivia, Austin, and Emily followed behind Evelyn.

"Oh, good. You're here." She walked over and hugged them. "Can't wait to meet your family, Austin."

"I'm warning you. We can be a bit boisterous." His eyes twinkled, and he kept an arm around Olivia's waist.

"Oh, Grams doesn't mind family chaos. Ours can be the same way," Emily assured him.

The doorbell rang. "Oh, they must be here." Donna hurried off to greet them.

Austin's family crowded through the door with a hubbub of laughter and teasing. He introduced each person as they entered. A pair of red-headed twins squealed when they saw Austin, and he scooped them up in his arms.

"And these two princesses are Ashley and Abby."

"Genevieve, I'm so glad to meet you." Donna took Austin's mother's hands in hers. "I adore your son."

"He's a good one." Genevieve nodded. "Your Livy and Austin seem to make a good couple. He couldn't stop talking about her last time he came to visit me."

"Come in. We're all out on the lanai. Let's get you settled into a chair and get drinks for everyone."

Heather and Jesse soon arrived with their son, Blake. And Patricia and Ted arrived with Cassandra. She still wasn't quite used to the idea that Ted was really her biological father, much less the fact he was dating her mother, but she was enjoying getting to know him.

Soon the party was in full swing. Everyone trekked into the kitchen and got plates of food and filtered back outside, sitting at the tables and chairs scattered around. The sun put on a showy display as it slowly sank in the sky, and the lanterns lit up as the sky darkened.

Emily sat at the edge of the lanai, playing with the twins. The little girls were totally taken with her, but then Emily was great with kids. She told Blake where to find the container of building blocks and he retrieved the blocks and sat with them, helping the twins build a castle.

Cassandra came over. "It's a great party, Donna."

"Thank you."

Cassandra nodded toward Ted and Patricia. "And what do you think about my uncle and your mom? You think it's serious?"

"I'm not sure. They seem happy. They're always together." Though, she had to admit it was strange to see her mother this happy. So relaxed. But, hey, if Ted and her mother had found each other again after all these years, more power to them. She had no idea if they'd just remain close friends... or if it would become something more.

"I'm not sure either. Uncle Ted seems so happy, though. Patricia came to dinner with us last night." They both looked over at Ted sitting at a table with Patricia and Heather and Jesse.

"So I heard you're staying at The Cabot Hotel."

"I am. I could stay with Uncle Ted, but he's basically turned the guest room into his study, so it seems easier to stay at the hotel." Cassandra blushed slightly. "And then... Delbert is there. He's escorting me to the wedding."

"He is? Great."

Cassandra's blushed deepened. "And... he asked me out on a date. Sunday, after all the wedding happenings are over. We're going out to dinner."

"That's wonderful." She'd seen a connection between Cassandra and Del when they were together.

"I... I admit I had a bit of a crush on him when I was young and he and his grandparents would come to the hotel each summer. Back then I'd always hoped he ask me out on a date, but we were just really good friends."

"So, now you finally get your date."

"I do."

"Fate is funny like that. Bringing people together again. Look at Ted and Patricia now, after all those years."

"I'm looking forward to it. A bit nervous, though. Which is silly, I guess. We're friends. Well, we were long ago. Good friends."

Donna smiled, but maybe Cassandra and Del would become more than good friends... just like maybe Ted and her mother might.

Cassandra excused herself to go over to talk

with Ted and Patricia. Barry came over and wrapped an arm around her waist, leaning close. "Looks like your party is a smashing success. It's nice to get to know the Woods family before the wedding."

"It is. His family is lovely. His mother? She's so charming. She does look a bit tired from the festivities, though, doesn't she?"

"A bit. But I see Wilson is keeping a close eye on her. Bringing her a drink. Staying by her side."

"His family all seems very close. I like that. I'm glad Olivia is marrying into a close-knit family."

"They do seem like nice folks." Barry nodded.

She heard the screen door to the lanai open and turned to see who was arriving. She'd thought everyone was here who'd been invited.

Her mouth dropped open in surprise. "Charlie…"

CHAPTER 4

"Dad. What are you doing here?" Olivia hurried up to Charlie. She'd sent him an email about moving up the wedding, but she hadn't expected him to show up. She hadn't even expected it for the original wedding date months from now.

She wasn't certain the last time she'd seen her dad. It had been years. Like lots of years.

"You didn't think I'd miss my little girl's wedding, did you?"

Well, actually she *had*.

"I came to give you away." Her father flashed his ever so charming smile.

Now *that* was a problem. She'd already asked Ted to give her away. Even though she'd only known Ted for a little while, she felt closer to him than to her own father, who had been notoriously missing from her life.

"I didn't think you'd come."

"Of course I'd come."

It was typical of her dad to show up unexpectedly, no advance warning, but she hadn't thought he'd bother with her wedding.

"I heard all the commotion back here, so I walked around back to see what's going on." He turned from her and walked up to her mother. "Donna, how've you been?"

"Just fine, Charlie." Her mother's voice was polite, but there wasn't a lot of warmth in it.

Not surprising. Her dad left when she was really young. She could barely remember him from that time. And she could probably count the times he'd visited on one hand... He'd left her mother alone to raise her and never sent any money to help.

"And who's this?" Charlie's voice boomed out as he pointed to Barry.

Barry looked a bit shocked as he stood with an arm around Donna's waist, watching the drama unfold.

"This is Barry, my husband," Donna said.

"So, you finally tied the knot, huh? Good for you. Hadn't heard that bit of news."

Olivia hadn't told Charlie when her mother and Barry got married. She figured if he wanted to stay out of Donna's life, then it wasn't any of his business if her mother married again, now was it?

Emily walked up to them. "Hey, so this is Charlie?"

"You bet. Your grandpa. I met you when you were just a wee thing."

A toddler, if Olivia remembered correctly. And Emily was seventeen now.

Emily looked at him skeptically. Her daughter always had been a good judge of character.

"And I should meet this fella you're going to marry." He turned back to face her.

"Austin. His name is Austin." She took a good long breath and turned to see Austin watching with interest.

It was always this way when Charlie came to town. He was loud, and a constant energy swirled around him. He demanded attention. The center of everything. Seemingly charming… at least to people who didn't know him well.

Only she wasn't sure she could deal with all of that right now. She smothered a sigh.

"Austin." She motioned for him to come over.

He crossed the distance and slipped an arm around her as he reached her side.

"Austin, this is Charlie. My... father."

"Good to meet you, sir." Austin held out his hand.

Charlie grabbed his hand, grinning, and pumped it vigorously. "Austin, huh? Great to meet you, son. Couldn't miss my little girl's wedding."

She wasn't a little girl, and Charlie had missed every big moment in her life. Why was he here now? But she smiled at him politely. She glanced over at her mother, who gave the tiniest shrug.

Charlie turned back to Barry. "So, you married my girl, Donna, huh? Made an honest woman out of her? I thought she'd just live out her life as an old spinster. She was always more married to that Parker's General Store than anything else."

Barry tightened his arm around her mother, and a disapproving expression crept over his features, quickly followed by a polite smile. Fake, but polite. Were they all going to just politely smile at Charlie all night?

"Charlie—"

He cut her off before she had a chance to tell him to be quiet. "She was my girl. I married her first, you know."

"Charlie, let's go talk." She grabbed his arm, hoping to drag him away before he said anything else outrageous. "Austin, I'll be back in a few minutes."

She led her father out of the screened enclosure and down to the dock by the waterway. She turned to face him, hands on hips. "Charlie, why are you here?"

"You're getting married." He shrugged. "Of course I'm here."

"Like you were for my graduation from high school? Or when Emily was born? Or for anything else big that ever happened in my life? Or anything little, for that matter. Or… really… just to stop by and see how I was doing?"

"Ah, Livy, don't be like that. You know I care about you." He started to take her hand, but she snatched it back.

"And how would I know that? Because you helped support me when I was a kid? Oh, that's right. You didn't. Because you kept in contact with me over the years? Oh, that's right. That's a big nope to that, too." Anger mixed with disappointment started to burn through her. She usually tried to ignore the fact that her father had all but abandoned her and her mother. But sometimes, especially since she'd had her own daughter, she couldn't imagine a parent just up and leaving their child.

"Hey, it's not like that. Donna said she had everything covered. A good job running the family business she got dropped into her lap. And... well, my jobs have kept me running all over the country."

"Mom has worked hard at the general store. Really hard. All the time raising me, then helping raise Emily. She wasn't *given* anything."

"Come on, Liv. You know what I mean. I didn't get things just handed to me like your mother did."

She counted to three. Then five. Then she glared at him, her hands balled into tight fists. "Charlie, I don't really want to get into all of that now. You're welcome to come to the wedding. But... I've already asked Ted Cabot to walk me down the aisle."

"And who the heck is Ted Cabot?" Charlie cocked an eyebrow.

She took a deep breath and squared her shoulders. "He's... Mom's father."

"What the heck?" Charlie's eyes widened. "But what about old Nelson? What does he think about that?"

"Charlie… Nelson died. And… look, it's a long story. Let's not get into it. But like I said, you're welcome as a guest."

"A guest. Not as father of the bride?" He looked more annoyed than hurt. "Fine. Whatever my little girl wants." His tone contradicted his agreeable words.

"In case you haven't noticed, I haven't been a little girl for a very long time. And Charlie? Be nice to mom. And cut out the remarks to Barry." She turned, her heart pounding, trying to get her emotions under control. She walked away, leaving him standing alone on the dock.

Why today? Why now?

Why had Charlie returned only to stir up trouble?

Donna sank onto the edge of the bed after the last of the guests left. She was unreasonably tired. Exhaustion settled on every muscle. The night had been a bit more than she'd planned.

Barry walked into the room. "I turned off

all the lights. Everything is locked up." He looked at her closely. "You okay?"

"I'm... just tired."

He sat on the bed beside her. "Is it Charlie coming to town?"

She leaned against him, and he wrapped his arm around her.

"Partly that. He's a complication I didn't expect for this wedding. He has a way of causing trouble when he comes to town. Not that coming to visit happens very often."

"He seems fairly sure of himself."

"You mean full of himself. Charlie is always that way. Loud. Trying to charm people with his smile and his whole good-guy persona."

"Yet, he left you alone to raise Livy."

"He did. Which was probably for the best. He was always so up and down. I never knew if he'd be the charming guy or the... not so charming one. And it would have been harder on Olivia if he'd stayed in her life even longer, then just up and left."

"He won't cause trouble at the wedding, will he?"

"I honestly don't know. I never know with Charlie." She sat there silently, remembering the anger and hurt when Charlie had left her alone with Olivia. Alone to raise her. Make a living. But at least the constant arguing was over when he disappeared. That had been a relief. No child needed to be around that much quarreling.

Barry reached over and tipped her chin up so she'd look at him. "I'm here, and I'll never leave you. And I'll do whatever I can to make sure nothing goes wrong at Livy's wedding." He kissed her gently.

The warmth of his kiss and the comfort of his support flooded through her, filled her. She placed her hands on his shoulders and kissed him back. Letting him feel her love. Showing how much she cared about him. There was nowhere she'd rather be right now than kissing this man.

He pulled away slightly and winked at her. "Hey, not bad for an old spinster lady, huh?"

She laughed. "I do adore you, you know."

"And I you, my love."

CHAPTER 5

Olivia knocked on the door to the teal cottage promptly at ten the next morning. Wilson opened the door. "Livy, there you are. Come in, come in."

She entered and looked around at the cheery room. Violet had done a remarkable job redoing all the cottages at the Blue Heron. Light spilled in the windows, and cute beach decor hung on the walls. Everything she'd done said 'come in, sit down, relax.'

Genevieve entered the room from the hallway looking refreshed and all smiles. "Livy, I'm so glad you could join me for tea. I thought we might sit out on the porch?"

"You two ladies go on out and take a seat.

I'll bring the tea." Wilson motioned toward the door.

They settled on two large wicker chairs with plump cushions. A light breeze blew in from the sea. Perfect weather. Hopefully it stayed this way for tonight's rehearsal.

Wilson brought out a tray with a teapot and two cups. "I'll let you two ladies sit and chat. I think I'll go wrangle up the twins and take them down by the water and do some sea shelling. Try to wear them out so they'll take a nap and not be so tired at the rehearsal tonight."

Genevieve poured them each a cup of tea, then leaned back in her chair. "I'm glad we're getting this time to talk. I know you're really busy, of course, but thank you for taking the time to come over this morning."

"I'm glad to have this break in the day. Some time to just sit and chat." She blew on her tea, then took a sip. "I'm hoping it's not all going to be too hectic. We tried to keep the guest list small, but it's hard when you've grown up in a small town and lived here your whole life." She worried that all these days of people and activities were too much for Austin's mom.

Genevieve smiled, looking perfectly calm and relaxed. "I'm sure it will all be perfect."

"We were so glad when Violet offered up the Blue Heron Cottages for the wedding. Tomorrow they'll put up a large tented area here in the courtyard."

"I think it will be lovely. And I'm glad you found a venue you like. You should have the wedding that you want." Genevieve paused, took a sip of her tea, and set the cup down on the table beside her. "I'm well aware that you two moved the wedding up because of me."

"Oh—"

Genevieve cut her off before she could protest. "No, I know that Austin wanted to... He wanted to make sure I could be at his wedding. It was gracious of you to move up the date."

"I'd do anything to make Austin happy."

"And I think you're a wonderful match for him. You do make him happy. I've never seen him this happy." Genevieve looked out at the courtyard, then back at her. "And I'm very glad to be able to be here. To be at his wedding. I... well, I don't know how many more big family events I'll get to be at. This disease... well... it's been a long, hard fight."

She reached out and touched Genevieve's

hand. "I'm so sorry for what you're going through."

Genevieve nodded and gave her a small smile. "We all have things that life throws at us that we wish we didn't have to endure. But... I'm a fighter, too. I'm doing my best to beat this. And... if the worst happens—if I have to *leave* —then I'm glad that Austin will have you by his side."

The right words wouldn't come. What to say to that? Pain washed through her at all that Genevieve had to go through. What her family was going through. The pain of not knowing if she'd be around to see her grandchildren grow up. See her other sons marry.

She brushed away a lone tear that trailed down her face. "I will be there if he needs me. But... we all hope that you can fight your way through this."

"I'm certainly trying." Genevieve picked up her teacup and put on a bright smile. "Now, let's talk about other, happier things. I hear you're wearing a wedding dress that has been in your family for generations."

She perked up some at the thought of Grace Parker's dress. "I am. And my cousin just wore it in her wedding. It makes me feel so connected to my family. To my ancestors. All the Parker women."

"That's such a nice thing to have. That connection." Genevieve nodded. "And your daughter is so charming. We had a nice long talk at Donna's last night. She told me all of her plans for college. Which colleges she was planning on applying to. Plus, she told me a lot of the history of Moonbeam."

"That's my Emily. Full of history. She does love it. And she is a great kid. I'm really lucky."

"Austin said that man who showed up at Donna's last night, he's your father?"

"Charlie." In spite of herself, a long sigh escaped. "Yes, he's my father. He was…" How to say it politely? "Not very present in my life. Like ever."

"I'm sorry."

She shrugged. "I guess I didn't know any difference. Mom was always there. I had plenty of love. Charlie is just someone who pops into my life every now and again. Usually without warning, like last night." She shrugged. "Austin is very lucky to have a father like Wilson."

A faraway expression settled on Genevieve's face for a few moments, then she turned and smiled. "Wilson is a wonderful father. Wonderful grandfather. Wonderful husband, too. I got really lucky when I met him."

"Where did you meet him?"

"Ah, that." A wide smile crossed her face. "My car ran out of gas right in front of his house. I got out of the car and just stared at it, not sure what to do. I was all dressed up from going to a bridal shower. High heels. Fancy dress. Anyway, he saw me standing there and came out to see what was wrong. He had some gas in his garage and filled up the tank enough for me to get to the gas station. But he followed me to make sure I got there."

The changing emotions flickering across Genevieve's face while she told the story warmed Olivia's heart and made her smile.

"Then, when he was sure I had a full tank, he came over and asked me out to dinner." She smiled softly. "That was the one and only time I've ever run out of gas. Just fate, I guess, to end up in front of his house."

"That is such a great story."

"The rest, as they say, is history. I fell in love with him... I think that very first day. We married a few months later. We had our ups and downs, like all couples do. I'm sure you and Austin will, too. But the thing is, we always promised we'd work through anything that life threw at us. And we have." Her voice lowered. "And I hope we'll make it through this health challenge, too."

With everything in her, she hoped that Genevieve would conquer her disease. Come out on the other side stronger and live a long, happy life. Austin's mother was such a remarkable woman. And she was just now getting the chance to get to know her. She hoped the fate that brought Genevieve and Wilson together would be kind to the Woods family and spare Genevieve.

CHAPTER 6

Cassandra headed down to the dining room for lunch. She'd grab a light meal. Maybe a salad. Then she'd have time to take a walk on the beach before heading up to get ready for Livy's rehearsal. She really missed beach walks when she was back home.

The hostess sat her at a table near the window, and she perused the menu, settling on a Caesar salad. She stared out the window while she waited for her meal.

"Cassandra, I thought I spied you in here." Delbert appeared beside her table.

She looked up at him and couldn't help the automatic smile that swept across her face. "Del, hi."

"Mind if I sit for a few minutes?"

"No, sit." She motioned to the chair across from her. "I'd love the company."

He sat down, relaxed, comfortable. Like he belonged here. But then, he did. He owned the place. A flicker of regret and loss crept through her. The hotel had once felt like that to her. That it was hers. That she belonged.

"What?" Del leaned forward.

She raised an eyebrow. What was he asking?

"You just look... sad."

She gave a little laugh. "Ah, I was thinking of when my family owned the hotel. Memories coming out of hiding, I guess."

"Is it hard on you seeing The Cabot now?"

"Not exactly. I'm thrilled you bought it and restored her. It was evident that my family wasn't ever going to make that happen. And it was sad to see the hotel deteriorate. It's just sometimes..." She shrugged. "I play the what-if game. What if Father and Uncle Ted hadn't argued? What if Uncle Ted wouldn't have left to go to Europe to take care of his wife? Just... a lot of what-ifs."

"But if we concentrate on the what-ifs... we miss where our choices have taken us. They've taken us to exactly where we are right now."

She smiled and nodded. "You're right, of course. And I have a good life now. Uncle Ted is back in it. I get to visit Moonbeam often to see him. I love my job."

"And I'm glad you get to visit often, too." His eyes twinkled as he said the words.

Only, she didn't know how to take it exactly. They had slipped back into being friends. And she was going to the wedding with him, and then dinner the next night. So maybe... they were more than just friends? Did he think of her that way?

Del laughed. "And now you have a million thoughts running through your mind. I can see it in your eyes."

He always had been able to know what she was thinking. When she was overanalyzing something.

"I was just..." She laughed. "Thinking."

"Of course you were." He gave her a knowing and accepting smile.

She should really concentrate on Del, not on her bouncing thoughts. Maybe she would ask him if he had time to take a beach walk with her.

"So, you have the rehearsal tonight."

Delbert reached for the iced tea the server brought him.

"Yes. Oh, and last night at Donna's? This man showed up. Evidently, he's Livy's father."

"Really?"

"I don't think he was expected. Patricia sure didn't have anything kind to say about him. I guess he basically disappeared right after Livy was born and rarely comes to town."

"That's unfortunate that Livy didn't have a father in her life."

"It is. I guess he's coming to the wedding, but Ted is giving Livy away. Or walking her down the aisle. Or whatever the proper term is for it now."

"Ted is?"

"Yes. Donna and Livy have gotten very close to Uncle Ted since they found out he's Donna's real father. I think Ted really enjoys having a family now. Something he never thought he'd have. And it broadened my family too, of course. I really like Donna, Livy, and Emily. Well, and Heather and Evelyn, too. And Patricia, of course." She laughed. "And all their spouses and or boyfriends. See how much my family has grown?"

"It has. You're very lucky."

She was lucky. And very pleased how things had turned out for her and Uncle Ted.

"So the rehearsal this evening, then a dinner?"

"Yes, they closed the Sea Glass Cafe for the night and we're having it there."

"So you'll get some of that great peach pie and ice cream, I bet." He grinned.

"Probably. Evelyn has worked out a special menu. I'm sure it will all be wonderful."

A worker hurried up to Delbert. "Sir, that call from London came in."

Delbert stood. "I'm sorry, have to go get this."

"No, go. That's fine."

He hurried away, and she watched his confident strides as he crossed the dining room. Smiling at customers. Saying hi to a server. A man in his element.

She turned to her salad, sorry to be eating alone, though she was certainly used to it. She ate most of her meals alone. Or occasionally she had dinner at one of the group homes with the kids. That was always fun, if chaotic.

Something always seemed to interrupt her time with Delbert. She only hoped nothing interfered with their dinner on Sunday.

She finished her lunch, then headed for the beach. Alone.

~

Violet set up the last chair for the rehearsal. Did she have enough seats? Though, maybe not everyone would sit. Did she have too many? Some people were in the wedding party, of course, so would they even sit down?

The arbor that Rob had made was beautiful, and tomorrow it would get decorated with fresh flowers. She frowned, wondering what she'd forgotten. It's not like she'd hosted a wedding rehearsal before.

Rob walked up carrying a large cooler. "I filled it with bottled water like you asked. That's probably a good idea in case any of the guests get thirsty."

"Ugh, that cooler is so old and beat up. I didn't even think of that."

"It's fine. It's just a cooler."

"It will have to do for tonight. Put it over there." She pointed off to the side. Then adjusted a row of chairs. Again.

"Come on, sis. Quit messing with them. Everything looks wonderful."

"Are you sure? I know tomorrow there will be flowers and bows and stuff. Doesn't it look a bit plain now?" She eyed the setup.

"It looks fine."

"Like you're some big expert on wedding rehearsals." She glared at him. "I think it needs something…"

"How about I get those two big pots of petunias you had me plant yesterday. I could put one pot on each side of the arbor."

"That would look nice." She nodded.

"The wedding party won't be here long, anyway. Just a quick rehearsal, then they're headed to Sea Glass Cafe for dinner."

She sighed. "I want everything to be perfect. This wedding is my first event. What if I mess stuff up? What if Livy isn't happy with it?"

He rolled his eyes at her… which annoyed her greatly. "What if everyone loves it? They will, you know. And they were very grateful to have this place to hold the wedding. And have you heard the Woods family talking? They love the cottages. Everything will be fine."

She frowned. "I hope so."

"Come on. Why don't you help me cart the flower pots out here?"

"No, I need to sweep the porches on the

extra cottages. Make sure they're all cleaned off and looking good."

"You swept them this morning. And you know no one is staying in those extra cottages, right?"

"Rob, quit second-guessing me. I want it to all go off without a hitch."

Her brother raised both his hands in surrender. "Okay, whatever you say. Just tell me what you need."

"Right now I just need those flower pots."

"As you wish." He disappeared off in the direction of the shed to retrieve the flowers.

She looked around the courtyard with critical eyes. It *did* look nice, didn't it? It had all been freshly mowed… well, the areas that had grass. She was still working on that. She'd trimmed bushes. Planted a couple of flower gardens nestled between the bushes for pops of color.

She went up to the front row of seats and adjusted them again, looking around quickly to make sure Rob didn't see her.

There were times when she doubted her whole decision to buy the cottages, renovate them, and open the small resort. Not that she'd ever let Rob know her doubts since he'd been so skeptical. She just wanted it to be a success. Start earning money. And she hoped like anything that she would enjoy running Blue Heron Cottages because it wasn't remotely similar to anything she'd ever done.

She chased her doubts away. She was certain she'd made the right decision to buy the cottages. Okay, ninety-five percent certain. Maybe even ninety-six.

She glanced at the row of chairs again. *Were they straight?*

Livy moved through the motions of the wedding rehearsal, not quite believing she was actually getting married. Everything had moved so quickly these last few weeks. So much rushing to get the wedding organized. Not exactly like she'd imagined planning her wedding. She thought she would be able to luxuriate in decisions and planning and every small detail.

And yet, she wouldn't trade doing all that if it meant that Austin's mother might not be at the wedding. She turned to see Genevieve sitting in a seat beside Wilson, a glowing smile on her face. Yes, all this was worth it.

Austin leaned over and kissed her. "You doing okay?"

She squeezed his hand. "I'm great."

"You know how much I appreciate you doing this, right?"

"Austin, I wouldn't have it any other way." She glanced over to where Heather was talking with the pastor. Everything had gone smoothly, thanks to Heather's help.

"Well, Livy. What a surprise." Charlie walked up to her. "I was out taking a walk. Thought I'd check out the venue. Didn't know you'd all be here."

Ah, maybe she should have invited him to the rehearsal. Guilt swept through her. Though it was just like Charlie to show up uninvited. She put on the now-familiar polite smile. "We're just finishing up the rehearsal. Then we're headed to Sea Glass Cafe for dinner. Would you like to join us?" *Please say no.* She didn't really want to deal with any stress or play interference between Charlie and her mother.

"That would be mighty nice." Charlie bobbed his head vigorously. "Get to know this young man better."

"Great." She tried to sound enthusiastic. Then felt guilty. Of course, she should have invited him to the rehearsal. What had she been thinking? He was her father. He deserved to be there.

Her thoughts and emotions about this man were so tangled, and she didn't think the day before her wedding was a very smart time to try to unravel it all.

People began to leave to head over to the cafe. "I'll see you at the cafe, then."

"Sure will." Charlie walked off, stopping to talk to Patricia and Ted.

She didn't miss the disapproving look on her grandmother's face. The complications were already starting. She let out a long sigh.

"It's going to be okay, Liv." Austin tucked her hand in the crook of his elbow.

"I'm sure it will." Though her voice didn't sound like she was very certain of her words. "And I want to go over and talk to Violet. Tell her how nice all this is. I think it's all going to work out perfectly. I'm so happy she let us have it here."

"It is nice, especially with my family staying here. Makes it easier on Mom."

She waved to Violet. "Come on. She's over there talking to Rob." She took his hand and they crossed the distance.

"I was so nervous about this." Violet laughed. "I know it's the bride that should be nervous, but it is my first big event here. This and the wedding tomorrow. I want everything to be perfect."

"It has been so far." She hugged Violet. "Just perfect."

"My sister has agonized over everything." Rob laughed as Violet sent him a dirty look.

"I did not." She laughed again. "Well, maybe I did."

"Did Evelyn already head out to the cafe?" Livy asked.

"She did. Wanted to make sure everything was ready." Rob nodded.

"I'm sure everything will be perfect with the dinner, too. She's doing a buffet at the cafe. Lots of good eating. And she's catering the wedding too, of course. I'll never figure out how she can balance so many things at once."

"And she makes it look easy." Rob's eyes widened in appreciation. "We should all probably head on over."

"I'll be there soon. I want to make sure everything is cleaned up here," Violet said as she headed over to start picking up the folding chairs.

She looked up at Austin. "You ready?"

"I'm ready. Let's have this rehearsal dinner. And then tomorrow? You'll become my wife." His eyes shone with love as he took her hand and they headed to the cafe.

CHAPTER 7

Donna looked over at where Charlie stood chatting with Heather and Jesse. Animated, as usual. Talking as if he wanted everyone to know he was here. How could anyone miss him?

Patricia came up beside her. "I don't see why Livy had to invite Charlie. It's not like he's really her father."

"Mother, of course he is."

"He was never here. Not for you. Not for Livy."

"But if Livy wants him here, he's welcome. Please don't make it difficult for her."

"I wouldn't." Her mother's eyes widened as if appalled by the suggestion.

But Donna knew how her mother could be

when she disapproved of something. Even if she'd softened a bit around the edges since dating Ted.

Charlie came striding up to the two of them, and she gave her mother a warning glance.

"There you two are. The matriarchs of this fine family. Looks like our little Livy is really going to get married." His voice boomed out, filling the room.

She never considered Olivia an *ours*. More of a *hers*. Her daughter.

"And you tied the knot, too. What is it with all you women getting married all at once? Heather there said she just got hitched, too."

"I guess they all found the right men for them," Patricia said pointedly.

"Yeah, well, I found Donna first. We were a good match for a while, weren't we, Donna?"

"Charlie, I don't think now is the time to talk about the past."

"Why not? We had a good past. Some really good times."

She tried to look back and think of even one good time with Charlie. There must have been some. When they were dating? Or first married? But for the life of her, she couldn't drag one good memory from the recesses of her mind. The brutal, hard reality of him leaving them had chased all hints of anything good far away.

Olivia stood by Austin, glancing over in their direction. The last thing she wanted was for Olivia to get upset. She forced herself to smile politely at Charlie.

Barry walked up to them, a matching civil smile on his own face. "Charlie." He nodded at him.

"Hey, Barney." Charlie grinned.

"Barry." Donna corrected, though she was certain he knew that.

"Right, Barry." Charlie dipped his chin. "Barry. I'll remember that. The one that took my Donna."

"Charlie, cut it out. I'm not your Donna. And please don't make a scene tonight. Or tomorrow."

"And keep your voice down," Patricia added with a frown, glancing around at the crowd to see if anyone was catching the conversation.

"I'm not making a scene, you are. You always were so dramatic about things." He gave Donna a dismissive look. One she remembered so keenly from their past.

Barry's arm wrapped around her waist as if

giving her support, but she glanced at him and shook her head slightly.

She wanted to handle this. This was her battle. She eyed Charlie sternly. "Charlie, I mean it. No trouble."

He held up both hands. "I'm not here to cause trouble. I'm just here to see our little girl get married."

Our. That word again. She gritted her teeth.

"And I still don't know why she asked that Ted guy to walk her down the aisle. I'm her father."

"Then start acting like one. Do what Olivia wants for her wedding. Be happy for her." Her tone came out harsher than she intended, but Charlie always seemed to bring out the worst in her.

"Of course, I'll do what she wants."

"Ted is a good man," Patricia said in defense. "He and Livy have gotten very close."

"You mean after the secret came out that he's Donna's father? Now that surprised me, Patricia. I mean, you having an affair? It was common knowledge that old Nelson cheated all the time, but you?"

"Charlie." She held up her hand. "You never know when to just leave things well enough alone, do you? I think maybe you should leave." She turned to her mother. "Mom, I'm sorry."

"You don't need to apologize for Charlie's behavior." Her mother glared at him with a look that could make grown men tremble. But not Charlie. He grinned back at her.

"I'm not going to leave unless my little Livy asks me to. But I do think I'll go check out some better company." He swiveled around and strode off toward Austin's family.

She let out a long sigh, and Barry pulled her closer. "You two Parker women stood toe to toe with that guy." He gave her an approving smile.

"Charlie is just…" She shrugged. "Charlie."

"I always thought the man was impossible. Never knew what you saw in him." Her mother shook her head.

"Looking back, I'm not sure what I did, either. But I did get Olivia out of that marriage. And for that, I'm forever grateful."

Olivia's shoulders tensed and hands balled into fists as Charlie approached where she and Austin were sitting and talking to Genevieve and

Wilson. What a ridiculous response to having her father near, but it was what it was.

"And this must be Austin's parents, right? Didn't get a chance to meet you at Donna's. I was... rushed off." He sent her a slightly accusing look.

She ignored it. "Charlie, this is Genevieve and Wilson, Austin's parents."

"Nice to meet you, Charlie." Wilson held out a hand.

Charlie pumped Wilson's hand. "Nice strong grip you got there, Wil."

"Wilson," she corrected.

"Right, Wilson."

"And Genevieve, you look all tuckered out."

"Charlie." She jumped up and placed her hand on his arm, giving Genevieve an apologetic look.

"What? She does. Maybe you kids are running her too hard. Lots of commotion for us old folks." He winked.

She glared.

"Thank you for your concern. But I'm fine," Genevieve said, always polite.

Wilson, on the other hand, was sending daggers toward Charlie and put a protective arm around Genevieve's shoulders.

"Looks like these kids planned this shindig in a hurry. I thought maybe Austin got my little girl prego and that's why they rushed the wedding."

"Charlie!" Olivia gasped out loud, and the burn of a blush covered her cheeks. "Stop it. I mean it."

"What?" He shrugged and gave her an innocent look.

Austin's face flashed with barely held back anger. Matched only by Wilson's fiery expression.

She grabbed her father's arm. "That's it. Come with me."

"What? Again? What did I do this time?" He still held firmly to his innocent look.

She ignored his protests and led him out of the cafe, whirling to face him as the door closed behind them. "Seriously? That's what you choose to say when you meet Austin's parents? For your information, we moved the wedding up so Austin's mother could be here. She's ill. That's why she looks tired. Not that any of this is any of your business."

"I just thought—"

She held up a hand. "I don't care what you thought. What you think now. All I want is for you to..." She swallowed, taking a deep breath, trying to control her anger. "I just want you to be like a *normal* father for once. Be supportive. Don't say outrageous things. Don't tick off Mom. I just want to be able to enjoy my wedding. I've never asked you for a single thing my whole life. But I'm asking this now. Is that too much to ask from you?"

To Charlie's credit, he did look a bit contrite. A *tiny* bit. "I don't mean to upset you."

"Well, you have." She glared at him.

"I'm sorry. I sometimes talk without thinking."

"I need you to think before you speak for the rest of the time you're here. Please, Charlie."

"Will do." He nodded slowly, then looked at her intently. "You don't like me very much, do you?"

She stared at him in surprise. "Charlie, I don't even *know* you. You caused that. You never came around."

"I told you. I traveled a lot for my job. I had responsibilities. I was busy."

"We make time for the people that are important to us." She stepped back. "If you come to the wedding tomorrow, do not make a scene. Stay away from Mom. And just... be nice."

She spun around and slipped back into the cafe, placing a careful smile on her face. Though when Austin looked at her, she knew she wasn't fooling him one bit.

Her mother walked over and took her hand. "You okay?"

"I'm fine." A lie, but she would be soon. She took a deep breath, calming her nerves.

"No, you're not. Did Charlie upset you?" Her mom searched her face.

"I took care of it. I think I set him straight. He said he'd be on good behavior tomorrow."

"Oh, honey. I'm sorry you have to deal with this. I don't want him to ruin your wedding. I could tell him to leave."

"No, it will be fine." She gave her mom a weak smile. Her mother wasn't fooled any more than Austin.

CHAPTER 8

Violet stood in the courtyard of the Blue Heron. The tent company had come and set up the two large, open-sided tents. She'd spent a good amount of time setting up chairs for the ceremony, making sure each row was even. Tables were set up in a second tent for after the ceremony. Then the first tent would be converted to a dance floor with a small, four-piece band playing music.

The florist came and draped flowers over the arbor with lots of greenery and ribbons intertwined. It really turned out lovely. It would be a beautiful backdrop for pictures.

Evelyn walked up. "Looks, great."

"Do you think so?" Violet scanned the setup again.

"I'm getting ready to put out these small baskets of flowers along the aisle. Then the centerpieces on the tables. We decided on lanterns for each table with small bowls surrounding them with a single blossom in each bowl."

"I can help with that," Violet offered eagerly. She had to do something with this nervous energy surging through her.

"You sure?"

"I'm positive." They placed the baskets along the aisle, and it did look truly beautiful. Then they made their way to each table and Evelyn showed her how to fill each bowl with clear marbles, then a bit of water, and float the blossoms.

"You've caught on quickly," Evelyn said.

"These make such a pretty table arrangement. Simple, yet lovely." Violet stood back and admired a table. "How do you know how to do all of this? Tell the florist how to do the arbor? Set up these table arrangements?"

"I've done about a million events, it seems like. I used to do them for the club." She shrugged. "That was back when I was married to Darren. But the club kind of exiled me after we divorced."

"I'm sorry."

"Oh, don't be." Evelyn smiled. "I find I don't miss it a bit. I still do some events now. I'm working on one next week at The Cabot. A fundraiser for the history museum."

"I don't know how you do it and stay so organized."

"I have a planner. Write everything down. After doing so many, it kind of becomes second nature. Each one is a little different, but still the same basics."

"If this wedding goes off well... I'm thinking of adding in weddings here at the cottages. Make it a wedding venue, too."

"That's a great idea."

"But I'm not sure I'd know where to even start. I can't afford to pay a wedding planner at this stage."

"I could help you. Teach you how to do things. I'll help you with the first wedding or two. After the first few, I bet you'll get it all figured out. I'll hook you up with my favorite florists. I know some caterers, or The Sea Glass Cafe can cater some simpler fare."

"I couldn't ask you to do all that."

Evelyn laughed. "You didn't ask. I offered.

Besides, I enjoy doing events. I really do. So you can't say no."

"Say no to what?" Rob walked up to them and gave Evelyn a special smile .

Yep, her brother was smitten, that's for sure.

Evelyn smiled back at him. "I was telling Violet that I'd help her if she wants to use the Blue Heron as a wedding venue, too. I'll get her started. Show her the ropes of planning events."

"Did she say yes? She's not very good at accepting help. Well, except from me when she needs something fixed around here."

She shot her brother a withering look. Not that he withered. "For your information... I did say yes. Well, I'm saying yes now." She turned to Evelyn. "I'd love your help. I'm a bit out of my league with weddings, but I'd love to offer them here."

"Perfect. Then together we'll figure them out. The best way to set them up. What size the venue can hold. What to do for small weddings or a bit larger ones. Don't worry, we'll sort everything out."

Violet hugged Evelyn. "I can't thank you enough." She turned to her brother. "I hope you appreciate how lucky you are to be dating this woman. She's a keeper."

"I know that." Rob slipped his arm around Evelyn.

Her brother might be a pain some of the time, but she liked seeing him this happy with Evelyn.

"I said you should ask her out. I was right, wasn't I?" She grinned as she started to walk away, but not before she caught Rob rolling his eyes at her.

"She always likes to think she's right."

She caught Rob's not-so-whispered words as she hurried away.

Livy stood in the mint cottage at the Blue Heron. Heather walked up behind her and wrapped her arms around her. "You look beautiful in Grace's wedding dress."

"I do love it. It's so special." She ran her hand along the delicate lace. "And I'm glad we could both wear it. I can't believe that after today we'll both be married." She turned to face Heather. "How did this happen? All so quickly?"

"I don't know, but I do know I'm ridiculously happy. Are you?"

"I am. I love Austin. And now that I've met his family, I adore them, too. And Emily is happy about me marrying him. Everything is just so…"

"Perfect?" Heather grinned.

"Yes, that's the word." She smiled back.

The door opened, and sunlight spilled inside, Emily hurrying in with it. "Mom, the guests are arriving. Can I get anything for you?"

"No, I'm almost ready."

"I saw Blake, and he wanted me to give this to you. Something borrowed." Emily held out a silver sand dollar necklace. "It's Grace's."

"Oh, that's such a thoughtful thing to do. And I don't have anything borrowed. I know it's a silly tradition, but… I want all of it. Something old, something new, something borrowed, something blue."

"Your shoes are new, and luckily I took care of the blue." Heather laughed and held out Olivia's shoes. "I painted the soles teal."

She laughed. "That's perfect. And the dress is old. I've got everything."

The cottage door opened again, and this time the spill of sunlight ushered her mother inside. She stopped in front of Livy, silent for a moment. Tears clouded her mother's eyes. "Oh, Olivia. You look so beautiful."

"Don't start crying," she warned her mother.

"I make no promises." Her mother took both of her hands. "I'm so happy for you. Austin is a wonderful man. I hope you'll both be very happy."

Evelyn popped her head in. "You about ready? The Woods family just got seated."

"Did you see any sign of Charlie?" Olivia asked, not sure if she wanted to hear that he was here… or he wasn't.

"Yes, he's out there. Sitting near the back." Evelyn nodded. "You ready?"

"I am." She put all thoughts of Charlie out of her mind. She had her wedding to think about, to enjoy.

She walked out of the cottage with the Parker women at her side, ready to marry the man she loved. Her heart filled with happiness. A day to remember forever.

The light breeze carried the scent of flowers and fresh salty air, mingled with a hint of the freshly mowed grass surrounding the courtyard. Grace's wedding dress rustled against her as if a caress from the past.

They waited while the twins scattered rose petals along the aisle, then she took Ted's arm and he gave her a quick kiss on the cheek. "You look so lovely."

She moved to the beginning of the aisle and saw Austin standing there under the flower-covered arbor. He looked up and saw her, and she held her breath, watching his emotions flicker across his face. His eyes filled with tears and she fought back tears of her own, her heart pounding thunderously in her chest.

Ted walked her down the aisle, dusted with petals, and Austin took her hands in his at the end, his eyes still glistening.

And before she knew it, they'd said their vows and the ceremony was over in a flash. Austin leaned forward and kissed her gently. "I love you. Thank you for making this happen so quickly," he whispered.

"I love you, too." She turned to see Genevieve with tears rolling down her cheeks. Wilson had a few of his own. And gratitude filled her for making this happen for all of them.

Austin beamed at her, his eyes full of love. They walked down the aisle together, and somehow she wasn't certain where she ended and Austin began. They were interwoven into a couple full of love and gratitude and happiness, surrounded by family and friends. There was no place she'd rather be.

CHAPTER 9

Donna and Evelyn stood at the edge of the tent canopy, watching the guests. "Livy looked so beautiful, didn't she?" Evelyn asked, though her eyes were on the tables of food.

"She did." Donna bumped gently against her sister. "And the food is fine. You're watching it like a hawk. There is more than enough."

Evelyn laughed. "I just want it to be perfect."

"It is. And that cake you made is beautiful. I love the shell topper. It's perfect for Livy." Donna looked across the crowd and spied the Jenkins twins with their heads close together, talking rapidly. She nodded their direction.

"Looks like Jackie and Jillian just found out some new scoop."

Evelyn looked over. "It does. It's a sure sign when they have their heads together like that. Wonder what their latest gossip is?"

"No telling." Donna scanned the crowd. "Have you seen Charlie? I hope he's not off causing trouble and he's not the subject of the twins' gossiping."

Evelyn turned and searched the crowd. "I don't see him. But then I don't hear any commotion that he's causing either." She laughed softly.

"Oh, wait. There he is." Donna nodded toward the far corner. "Over talking to Cassandra and Delbert. I think I'll wander over there and make sure things are okay."

"I could do that for you."

She sighed. "No, Charlie is my problem. I'm the one who brought him into the family." She threaded her way through the crowd.

"Ah, here's the mother of the bride. My beautiful Donna." Charlie tossed out his mischievous grin.

"Knock it off, Charlie." She turned to Cassandra and Del. "Are you two having a good time?"

"We are. It's a lovely wedding. And I predict Violet is going to make quite a success of the Blue Heron Cottages. The resort has turned out so lovely." Cassandra smiled at her, politely ignoring her sharp remark to Charlie.

"Yes, it's a great wedding and Livy looked beautiful," Del added.

"So, Cassie here." Charlie barged into the conversation, nodding toward Cassandra. "I think I have her figured out. She's your new daddy's niece, right?"

Could the man ever quit making inappropriate remarks? She shook her head, hoping he'd take a hint.

"Ted is my uncle, yes." Cassandra nodded.

"Well, you all got yourself quite the family then. Marrying into all these Parker women. They're a bit headstrong, but I guess you've noticed."

"I adore being part of their family." Cassandra sent her a reassuring look.

"And old Patricia. Sly old fox, huh? Having an affair with your uncle."

Cassandra's eyes widened.

She glared at Charlie. "Charlie. We're not going to talk about any of this. Got it? It doesn't involve you. Just drop it."

"I just wondered if Cassie here knew what she was getting herself into. It's hard to break into the Parker circle. I'm proof of that."

Donna stood with her mouth open, not sure how to reply to that. "Charlie, you were welcomed into the family from day one. But you chose to leave. You left your baby daughter. You shouldn't expect to get a big welcome when you came back to town after that." She turned to Cassandra and Del. "I'm sorry."

"Hey, don't go apologizing for me. I just state things as they are."

"Charlie, can we not do this now? It's Olivia's wedding."

"Right, my daughter." His voice rose. "And I didn't even get to walk her down the aisle. That Ted guy that everyone thinks is so great took my place."

"Charlie. That's enough." Patricia's voice came from behind her.

She swiveled to see her mother standing there, hands on hips, eyes flashing.

"This isn't about you." Patricia pointed her finger at Charlie. "It's Olivia's day. Lower your voice. If you're displeased about things, you should leave. As a matter of fact, I think it would be best if you *do* leave."

"You can't tell me what to do." Charlie glared at Patricia.

"It's a very strong suggestion."

"I'm staying. Unless Livy wants me to leave."

"I… I do." Olivia walked up and stood by her and Patricia. "I'd like you to leave now, Charlie. Please don't spoil my day. Thank you for coming, but now… it would be best if you leave. I asked you not to upset anyone. And you have. Please… just leave."

"You don't mean that."

"I think she does." Heather came up to stand beside them, with Evelyn at her side. It was like the Parker women had an instinct when one of them needed support.

"You Parker women. Never could figure out what makes you so uppity." Charlie scowled. "Fine, I'll leave. I just wanted to enjoy my daughter's wedding, but it's obvious I'm not welcome here." He spun around and stalked off.

All the Parker women stood there, watching him leave.

When he'd finally disappeared, Donna turned to all of them. "Now, let's go celebrate. This is Livy's big day."

Olivia leaned over and kissed her cheek. "Thanks for always being there for me, Mom."

"There's nowhere I'd rather be." She squeezed her daughter's hand. "Now, go find your husband. Enjoy yourself."

Cassandra stood with Del as the Parker women all scattered back into the crowd and the tension floated away on the gentle gulf breeze. "That was interesting. That Charlie fellow is really something," Cassandra said.

"He is. But… he's no match for the Parker women, is he?"

Cassandra laughed. "No, he's not."

"Any chance you'd like to slip away from the crowd for a bit and take a walk on the beach?"

"I'd love to." They walked out from under the tent and slipped their shoes off near the palm trees lining the edge of the beach. Delbert rolled up the bottom of his slacks, then took her hand. They walked silently to the water's edge. The warm water covered her feet in foamy white bubbles from the edge of the waves, whispering a lullaby, soothing and slow.

"Ah, this is nice." She stood in the water, looking out at the stars twinkling overhead.

"It is." Del slipped his arm around her.

"Families sure can be complicated, can't they?" she asked, watching the moonlight dance across the waves.

"They can be." He nodded agreeably.

"I feel bad for Donna and for Livy. Sorry they never had Charlie's support. That he's a bit of a troublemaker when he does come to town."

"But they have the rest of their family. They have you and Ted now, too. They really are lucky."

She smiled at him. "I guess you're right."

"You want to sit for a bit?"

She nodded and sank down on the cool sand. He dropped down beside her and took her hand in his again. It was so quiet and peaceful sitting and watching the waves roll to shore.

"I'm having a nice time with you tonight." Del's words rolled over her just like the incoming waves. "I thought we'd never get some time alone again."

"It is nice." Her words were barely audible over the pounding of her pulse.

He was looking at her closely. Very closely.

She was certain... *almost certain..* that he was going to kiss her.

He leaned closer to her—

"Hey, you guys. Did you come out to escape the crowd, too?" Emily and Blake stood next to them in the moonlight. "We thought we might take a quick walk on the beach. But Heather texted and they're getting ready to cut the cake. You don't want to miss that, do you?"

Her thoughts ping-ponged around. Had he been getting ready to kiss her? Had she imagined that? And what had Emily just said? Something about a cake?

Delbert stood and reached down a hand. "No, we don't want to miss the cake cutting. You're right."

She placed her hand in his strong one as he pulled her to her feet. She brushed the sand from her dress. "No... we don't want to miss that." Though she really did. She wanted to be alone with Delbert. She wanted to sit back down on the sand and see if Delbert was finally —*finally*—going to kiss her.

Instead, they trailed behind Emily and Blake, headed back to the celebration, the moment lost, leaving her wondering...

Olivia and Austin stood out on the deck of his home late that evening, unwinding from their wedding day. She'd loved every moment of it. The ceremony. Laughing with friends and family. Dancing with Austin. Watching Austin dance with a twin in each of his arms. The day had been perfect.

It still was perfect. The light from an almost full moon spilled over the waves. Stars twinkled up in the sky. She closed her eyes and breathed in deeply. Right here with Austin was home. The very perfect moment would stay etched in her memory forever.

They were spending the night at Austin's house because he didn't want to leave town while his family—his mother—was still here. They promised each other they'd take a proper honeymoon soon. But there was no place she'd rather be than right here with him. It didn't matter where here was.

One thing they hadn't figured out in their rush to get married was their living situation. If Austin would move in with Emily and her at her house. Though it really was small for the three of them. Or if they'd try to find a new place to live. But for tonight, they were staying at the house he was renting on the beach, enjoying being alone.

They shed their shoes, and Austin unbuttoned the top buttons of his shirt. A light breeze blew her hair away from her face. She stood at the railing with Austin behind her, his arms encircling her.

"So was the wedding all you'd hoped for?" he asked.

"And more." She leaned back against him and he tightened his hold, kissing her neck.

"Are you upset about your father?" He spoke softly against her.

"No, not really. I refuse to let anything or anyone spoil this day. It was perfect." She turned to face him. "Everything was perfect. And your mother looked so happy."

"She did." He kissed her gently. "I'll never forget this day."

She reached up and touched his face. "I love you, you know."

"That's a good thing because I heard a rumor that we just got married." He grinned at her. "Now, what do you say, Mrs. Woods? Would you care to go to bed with your new husband?"

"Well, Mr. Woods, I think that is the most excellent plan." She smiled at him, took his outstretched hand, and they walked back into the beach house, side by side.

CHAPTER 10

Olivia opened her eyes as the bright sunshine streamed into the room. It took her a moment to remember where she was. She reached out a hand, but Austin's side of the bed was cold. She scooted up in bed, clearing her mind, and leaned back against the pillows.

Austin walked in with a tray in his hands. "Good morning, Mrs. Woods. I thought you deserved breakfast in bed." He settled the tray next to her and climbed in beside her. "I know you need your coffee. And I picked up cinnamon rolls yesterday for this morning. All I had to do was heat them up. See what a good planner your husband is?"

She leaned over and rewarded him with a

kiss. "Yes, he's a keeper. Anyone that brings me coffee is okay in my book."

She drank her coffee and munched on a cinnamon roll, still amazed that she was married to this man.

"So, now what?" he asked as they finished up.

"We're headed to the Blue Heron. I was talking to your sisters about having a nice beach day. They're going to send your brothers to Sea Glass Cafe to get a picnic for everyone."

"That's how you want to spend your first honeymoon day?"

"It sure is. So you better get moving, mister. And don't use up all the hot water." She grinned at him.

An hour later, they pulled into the drive at Blue Heron Cottages. The twins were out on a porch and squealed in delight when they saw Austin. "Uncle Austin. We're gonna go to the beach. Will you play with us? We want to jump the waves. Momma said we can only do that if we're holding a grownup's hand," one of the twins said.

The other twin looked at him seriously. "Are you a grownup?"

Austin laughed out loud. "Well, occasionally."

The whole family headed to the beach and put up a couple of popups for shade. Wilson, Austin, and his brothers took the twins into the water. His sisters went off shelling. Olivia sat in the shade with Genevieve.

"This is a wonderful way to top off a wonderful time here in Moonbeam." Genevieve watched her husband, sons, and granddaughters cavort in the waves for a few long moments. Then she turned to her. "I'll never forget this."

It was impossible to miss the longing and melancholy in her eyes. A look like she was trying to sear the memory in her mind.

"I will never forget your kindness in moving the wedding up. I'll remember always seeing his tears when he first saw you yesterday. I hope you two have a long and happy marriage with lots of blessings."

"Oh, Genevieve." She fought back tears. This strong woman was facing life head-on and treasuring every moment she had. A woman to be admired.

Genevieve patted her hand. "No, don't feel sorry for me. I've had a wonderful life. I hope I'm blessed with many more years, but if that's not in the plans for me, I'm still grateful for all I have."

Wilson jogged up to them and grabbed a towel. "You doing okay, Momma?"

"I'm doing fine. Why don't you come sit with me for a bit and let Livy go play with the kids."

Wilson plopped down beside Genevieve. "Sounds like a plan. I swear those twins exhaust me... not to mention your sons."

"Oh, they're my sons today, are they?" Genevieve smiled.

"Well, you usually claim them when they aren't causing trouble and say they're mine when they are." Wilson laughed.

Livy rose. "I guess this means it's my turn to go play in the waves." She walked toward the shoreline, looking back to see Genevieve and Wilson talking, their heads close together. She swallowed and sent up a prayer that they'd have many more years of those quiet moments together.

Cassandra wanted to roll her eyes at herself as she got ready on Sunday evening. She'd changed outfits four times. Shoes three times. And she couldn't decide on which jewelry to wear. She'd decided to let her hair stay down, loose on her shoulders. So at least *one* decision had been made.

She eyed the clothes hanging in the closet and spread out on the bed, then down at the simple teal dress she had on. She glanced at the clock. It was really time to make a decision. She'd wear this dress.

Yay, another decision.

Three more bracelets tried on, two pairs of earrings, and two changes of shoes, and she had her outfit.

It was silly to be this nervous. There was no hiding from it. She was nervous. She and Delbert had been friends for years, granted, with a huge break in the middle. But she'd always been so comfortable with him. Talking was easy with him. So, yes, what she was feeling now was foolish.

She dutifully tried to talk herself out of feeling this way. To no avail.

Tonight her heart was skittering around like a drop of water on a hot skillet. And nothing she said to herself did a thing to calm her nerves. The anticipation, all day long, had stretched her to her limits.

She chewed her bottom lip. With one last look in the mirror and a frown meant to convince herself to get over herself, she headed downstairs to meet Delbert.

For their date.

She had an actual, honest-to-goodness date with Delbert Hamilton. That thought did nothing to quiet her nerves.

When she entered the lobby, Delbert looked up from where he stood by the reception desk, and a wide smile spread across his face. Her pulse quickened and she swallowed. *Get it together, woman. It's just a simple date.*

But it felt like so much more.

He strode across the distance and took both her hands in his warm grip. "You look lovely."

"Thank you." The heat of a blush flushed her cheeks. Did he notice? He looked so handsome in crisp slacks and a blue button-down shirt with the cuffs slightly rolled up.

"I can't believe we're finally having our first official date. You've kept me waiting a lot of years." The grin he gave her also did nothing to soothe her jangled nerves.

He led her into the private dining room. Yellow roses adorned the table as well as another bouquet sitting on the large windowsill. A smile swept across her face.

She turned to him. "The yellow roses. They're my favorite. Did you remember that all these years?" She, herself, remembered so many little details about Del. It surprised her. How his smiles spread to his eyes. That blue was his favorite color. That he loved to read thrillers, or at least he used to.

"I was hoping they still were." He smiled— and, yes, his eyes lit up—looking pleased with himself. "And the chef made a special dinner for us. It should be served in about thirty minutes. I thought we could have drinks first."

She nodded, and he poured glasses of wine, then walked her over to the large windows overlooking the bay. He raised his glass. "To finally having our dinner."

She gently clinked her glass against his. *Finally* was right. She'd dreamed about going out on a date with Del that last summer he'd come to The Cabot. And she'd hoped he'd ask her out when he came back the next summer... only he never showed up. But now? Now, here they were. Together. On a real date. Only thirty-ish years since she'd first dreamed of it.

They stood for a bit, watching the boats slip

past in the bay. She was suddenly at a loss for words as they stood in uncharacteristically awkward silence.

Del gave a little laugh. "We seem to be a bit... quiet. Which is silly since you're always so easy to talk to."

"Maybe because we've officially called this a date?" She gave him a tentative smile, hoping something would break the tension between them.

"Maybe." He nodded. "So... let's talk like we both just happened to drop by here at the same time. Oh, hello, I'm so surprised to see you here." He gave her an impish grin.

She laughed. "That might work."

And just like that, they settled into their normal, easy conversation, interrupted only by their delicious dinner being served. As they finished their meal, a knock sounded at the door.

"Come in," Delbert called out.

The manager of the hotel stood at the door. "I'm sorry to bother you, sir... but there's a problem. I know we weren't supposed to interrupt."

"You can't handle it?"

"I, uh... handled it. But... there was a fire. I

thought you should know."

Del jumped up. "A fire? Where?"

"In a suite on the ground floor. Seems like one of our guests didn't feel like the no-smoking rule applied to him. Fell asleep and caught the bedspread on fire. There's smoke damage, and the EMTs are checking him out now. The sprinklers came on and... well, it's quite a mess."

"Go." She nodded at Del, knowing he wanted to go check things out for himself.

"I'm sorry..." A torn expression clung to his face.

She rose and walked over to him. "No, that's fine. And... thank you. I had a wonderful time."

He squeezed her hand, a worried look on his face, then hurried after the manager.

She picked up her wine glass, took one last sip, then headed up to her room. Disappointment rolled through her. This was not exactly how she'd planned for the evening to end. She'd hoped they might have a nightcap out on the porch overlooking the bay. And maybe, just maybe, he'd kiss her. A kiss she'd been waiting thirty years for.

CHAPTER 11

Del ran into Ted in the lobby of the hotel the next day. "Hi, Ted. What brings you here?"

"I'm meeting Cassie. Picking her up and we're going to walk to the wharf and have lunch at Jimmy's."

He'd hoped to have lunch with Cassandra himself today, but it looked like Ted had beaten him to it. He wanted to apologize to her for leaving so abruptly last night. But he'd been too busy to even call her this morning. The room with the fire was going to need a total redo. He'd gotten a fire restoration company in, and they were doing their thing. The smoke smell had permeated so much. He was having the room repainted and fresh carpet put down. The mattress had been destroyed. But thank goodness the foolish man hadn't been harmed, or worse, killed. He'd walked away with a minor burn on his arm.

City inspectors had been out to confirm the rest of the hotel was in no danger. Insurance company had been out. So many phone calls. His morning had been crazy busy.

He brought his attention back to Ted, pushing away the troubles of the hotel. "Well, I hope you have a good time."

"I hear you and Cassie had an official date last night." Ted nodded approvingly. "She seemed pleased about it. Did you have a good time?"

"We did… but I got called away early. Hotel emergency."

"Ah, the fire. I heard about it." Ted shook his head. "The whole town knows about it by now."

"There's some damage, but no real injuries. It could have been much worse."

"That's good. But sorry your date got cut short. Frankly, I'm glad to see Cassandra dating again."

He raised his eyebrows. "She hasn't been?" He figured her nights were peppered with dates back home. She was smart, pretty, talented. Why wouldn't she be dating all the time?

"Ah... well... she *had* dated. One guy for quite some time. Vincent. Seemed like a nice enough fellow. I believe Cassandra cared about him. They dated for a few years. I thought they might even get married."

He waited, wanting to know what happened. Cassandra hadn't ever mentioned a long-time boyfriend.

"She found out—quite unexpectedly—that he was cheating on her. She came back early from a trip to California. Called his office and his secretary said he was at their favorite restaurant. She decided to drop by to surprise him. Only she was the one who got surprised. He had his arm around another woman, kissing her. Evidently, she found out after the fact that it wasn't the first."

"Oh, that's too bad." Poor Cassandra, to be tricked like that. Cheated on.

"She felt very foolish. And so angry. She thought she should have known. Sensed it or felt it. She's been a bit... distrustful... of men since then. You're the first man she's dated since Vincent."

Pleasure seeped through him that Cassandra felt she could trust him. And of course, she could.

"Anyway, it goes without saying, I guess... don't hurt her." Ted pinned him with a look that said he meant business.

"I won't. I wouldn't. I... care about her."

"Good, that's what I wanted to hear. And I'm glad you're taking it slowly. She might be a bit... skittish."

"I don't blame her."

"I don't either. And I know I'm being the overprotective uncle... but I do adore her and only want the best for her. So just... don't..." Ted shrugged.

"Don't worry. I won't. She means a lot to me."

Ted nodded. "Okay then. Enough of the man-to-man talk. I better go up and get Cassie for our lunch."

"Have fun."

He turned when the manager came up to him. "Sir, the restoration company wants to talk to you."

"Okay, thanks." He hurried off to the

damaged room. He wanted to talk to Cassandra more than ever now. Assure her that she was a priority for him and apologize for leaving her alone last night. Maybe he'd get a chance after she got back from her lunch.

CHAPTER 12

"Violet, you've swept that porch like three times." Rob rolled his eyes at his sister standing on the porch of the teal cottage.

"I have not." She glared at him.

"It's all going to be okay. The wedding was a success. Everyone loved the Blue Heron. You've done a great job. This grand opening week will be great, you'll see."

"You're just saying that because you're my brother."

"No, actually, I'm very proud of you. You've really turned this place around from the dumpy Murphy's to the refreshed and renamed Blue Heron Cottages. I know I wasn't very supportive at first."

"You think?" She raised an eyebrow.

"Well, I came around." He took the broom from her hand. "But I swear, you're driving me crazy with this restless energy. What time do you think the first guests will arrive?"

"Check-in is three p.m., but maybe some will come early?" She shrugged and tried to yank the broom from his hand. He held it out of reach, high above his head.

"You've cleaned the rooms. Made the beds. Watered the flowers in front of each cottage. And don't think I didn't see you washing the windows on the orange cottage, yet again."

"I don't have an orange cottage." She stood with her hands on her hips, a defiant look on her face.

"Then what's that one?" He pointed to the *obvious* orange cottage.

She sighed. "That's peach, not orange."

He shrugged. "Looks orange to me."

"Don't call it that. I've named each cottage for its color and there's a sign on each one. There is no *orange* cottage."

"Whatever you say, sis."

"I say give me back that broom."

He handed it to her. If it kept her busy until the first guests arrived, he guessed there was no harm in her sweeping the porch for the bazillionth time. "I'm going to go make us a late lunch."

"I'm not hungry."

"I'm making you a sandwich. Come in and eat it." He gave her a listen-to-your-brother look.

She sighed. "Okay. But what if someone comes?"

"You'll hear them pull up. Or we can eat on the front porch if you'd rather."

"Fine. I'll come eat. But then I need to get back out here and make sure everything is perfect."

He rolled his eyes once again. Everything was more than ready for Violet's first official guests. She just wouldn't admit it. He hoped it didn't take long until she calmed down a bit about running the resort. She'd handled everything at Livy and Austin's wedding like a champ. He wasn't sure why she was so nervous now. But then his sister was often a mystery to him.

Evelyn packed up baskets of baked goods after the lunch crowd slowed at Sea Glass Cafe. One basket for each cottage at the Blue Heron. She wanted to surprise Violet with goodies for her guests on her big opening day.

She turned to Melody. "Will you be okay for a bit? I want to deliver these to Violet."

"I'll be fine. Emily will be in soon to work."

"I'll be back soon. Oh, and Ethan is still out there in the cafe. Looks like he might need more tea."

"Okay, I'll get that." Melody headed out of the kitchen.

Evelyn grinned. Ethan came in almost daily, and he only had eyes for Melody. But she was oblivious to his attention. Maybe someday he would actually get up the nerve to ask her out. Maybe.

She loaded up her car and headed over to the cottages to deliver her baskets. As she pulled into the drive, Violet was standing near the door to the owner's cottage, talking to Rob. Rob smiled when he saw her and waved.

"So, how's the opening going?" she asked as she walked up to them.

"Check-in officially is three p.m.," Violet said. "But, of course, I'm ready whenever our first guest comes. The cottages are all cleaned after Austin's family left this morning. It was a nice trial run with just a few cottages filled and the wedding. After your offer to help, I'm going to be adding weddings to our website. You know, after I get the whole running the cottages sorted out. But the wedding worked out well, didn't it?"

"It did. And I think this would be a lovely venue for weddings. Livy's sure was wonderful. It looked magical with the lights strung in the tent and the pretty flowers and the lanterns on each table."

"I'm hoping that I can keep the cottages full most of the time. Recoup some of the expense of rehabbing the place."

"How full are you this week?"

"I've got four cottages rented for the week. And then one more for next weekend."

"That sounds promising." She motioned back toward her car. "I brought welcome baskets for you. They're in the back of my car."

"That's so nice of you, thank you. I'll get them and put them in the cottages." Violet headed toward the car.

Rob took her hand and led her over to a bench under a trio of palm trees. "That was really nice of you to bring welcome baskets for my sister."

"I wasn't sure how many she'd need. If she only has four cottages rented, there'll be some extra."

Rob grinned. "Perfect. Then there'll be some left for me."

"Or you could come by the cafe for dinner tonight. I'll save you a slice of peach pie."

"I think I'll stick around here tonight. Violet is nervous about the opening. I want to be around just in case. Help her out. Maybe cart suitcases or something. She's so nervous. She spilled coffee all over this morning. Dropped a plate and broke it." He shook his head. "I tried to tease her out of it, but no luck."

"The wedding was lovely, and Austin's family raved about how cute and comfortable the cottages were. I'm sure she'll make a great success of her venture."

"I hope so."

"How's the writing coming?"

"Great. Finally. I've been getting up really early every morning and writing. Then I take a break, then go back and revise. Kind of getting into a rhythm here."

"I'm happy for you."

"No kidding. That writer's block I had was not fun." He trailed a finger along her arm. "I keep thinking Violet is going to toss me out of the cottage. Though, I do make the coffee, so she's happy about that."

"She wouldn't throw you out. She probably likes having you around."

"Mostly." He shrugged. "Anyway, she can't really afford to hire any help yet, so I'm sticking around."

Reluctantly, she rose. "I really need to get back to the cafe."

He stood and took her hand, pulling her close. "How about you get a thank you kiss for the baskets?"

She grinned. "I don't think Violet wants to kiss me."

"Oh, I'm volunteering to do it for her." He winked, then settled his lips on hers.

Her heart did a double beat. She still wasn't used to the idea of dating someone. But Rob made her very happy. They spent hours talking. He even came by the cafe sometimes after hours and helped her close up. He was comfortable to be with, yet her heart did a little flutter every time she saw him. You'd think by her age she'd be over that kind of thing…

"I know I'm busy with the cottages and you

said Livy is supposed to be taking time off this week…"

"Which she won't." She shook her head. She'd give it until *maybe* tomorrow before Livy showed up. Wouldn't be totally surprised to see her show up tonight.

"You think we could find time soon to go on a date? Or even spend time at your apartment? I'd say we could meet here, but things are a bit crazy right now."

"That sounds wonderful. Maybe after Livy comes back to work full time?"

"I'll try to be patient." He kissed her again. "But I don't plan on waiting until then to see you. I'll be by for some of that pie tomorrow."

He walked her back to her car, and she waved to Violet, who was sweeping off the deck of an already spotless cottage. One more quick kiss and she slipped into the car, a small smile on her face. She was getting used to his kisses. And the way he listened to her and accepted her just like she was, not wanting her to change.

She eagerly awaited their date—when they finally could make it happen—and hopefully, she wouldn't be too busy to chat a bit if he dropped by the cafe tomorrow.

Donna and Barry sat out on the lanai that night, enjoying some chamomile tea. She'd pretty much converted him to a chamomile drinker on their nights sitting outside. Their special time together. They'd chat about their days and catch up.

"So I was certain that Livy would come into the cafe today. But, surprisingly, she stayed away." Donna smiled. "I guess she really is honeymooning at Austin's."

"You all recovered from the wedding festivities?" Barry stroked her hand as they sat there.

"Pretty much. Even though we planned it all in just a few weeks, it was wonderful, wasn't it?"

"It was." He squeezed her hand.

She turned to look when the screen door to the lanai creaked open, and her mouth dropped open when she saw Charlie. "You can't just come walking around back, Charlie. This isn't your house anymore."

"It was." He shrugged, dismissing her remark. "I was looking for Livy. Figured she might be here. Her house is dark."

"She's on her honeymoon." She gritted her

teeth, annoyed at the interruption. Annoyed that Charlie thought it was okay to just keep walking into her home. Into her life.

"Thought she said they weren't going anywhere."

"They didn't. They're just spending some time alone."

"Then where is Emily?"

"She's staying with us, but she's off with friends now."

"I'm sure not getting much time with my family this trip to town."

"Olivia has been busy with her wedding and honeymoon, Charlie."

Barry gave her hand a firm squeeze of support.

"Well, I came a long way to see them."

Typical Charlie. Always about him. "I'm sure Olivia appreciated you coming. When I see her again, I'll tell her you stopped by."

"You'd think she'd at least call me and set up some time for us to talk for a bit."

"Maybe next time you come to town it won't be quite so crazy busy." Not that she thought he'd come back again very soon. He never did.

"Tell her I'm looking for her."

"I'll do that, Charlie. Good night."

Charlie scowled and disappeared back out the doorway. She let out a long breath. "That man…"

"He's a bit much, isn't he?" Barry said agreeably.

"That's an understatement." She took a sip of her tea, hoping it would soothe her, then turned to Barry and grinned. "You know what the good thing is?"

"No, what?"

"Every time Charlie shows up it reminds me how impossibly self-centered he is and makes me appreciate you all the more." She laughed.

"Well, then. The guy is welcome here any time." He grinned, then leaned over and kissed her.

And she forgot about Charlie. Forgot about everything except how lucky she was to have Barry in her life and how much she loved him.

CHAPTER 13

Cassie sat out on the porch of The Cabot after getting back from her lunch with Uncle Ted. She wasn't sitting there in plain sight, hoping that Del might see her. That wasn't it at all. They just had really good sweet tea at The Cabot was all. But her drink was almost gone, and no sign of Del. She didn't want to bother him if he was really busy. He did have a hotel to run. And there was the whole fire thing.

She took the last sip and set the glass on the table beside her. Now what to do? The afternoon stretched out before her.

"There you are." Del hurried up to her. "I told my manager to keep an eye out for your return. He said he saw you head out here. I wanted to talk to you."

Suddenly the afternoon looked brighter. Maybe she could convince him to take a little break and walk along the harbor? She motioned to the chair beside her. "Sit down. How's the room? Is there a lot of damage?"

"Some. Well, lots. But we'll repaint and get new furniture and carpets. Hope it will only take a month or so to get everything in. Should be all set for January when the snowbirds come to town and we get busy again."

"And the guest? Is he okay?"

"Yes, a minor burn. He apologized over and over... not that it makes it any better. Some people just don't think the rules apply to them. No smoking anywhere inside the hotel." He frowned as he shook his head.

"I'm glad it wasn't worse."

"Me, too. Anyway, I wanted to say how sorry I am that our dinner got cut short." He took her hand in his and a wave of warmth and connection flowed through her.

She stared down at their hands, then remembered she hadn't answered him. "I was sorry, too." So very sorry. She'd wanted handholding and long conversations and maybe a goodnight kiss. *Not* a hotel emergency.

"So, how about I make it up to you? I'll cook dinner for you tomorrow night?" He looked at her expectantly.

"That would be nice." *Nice? Nice?* It would be *fantastic* to have some more time alone with him. What was wrong with her when she got around Delbert?

"Six? I should be done with work by then."

She nodded, afraid she'd say something silly like nice again.

He glanced down in annoyance at his phone pinging with text messages. "I'm sorry. I have to go. An electrical problem on the first floor. Might be related to the fire."

Disappointment blasted through her, though she put on an encouraging smile. "Go. That's fine." So much for spending more time with him and her dream of a nice harbor walk.

"I'll wrap all this up and I promise we won't be disturbed tomorrow night."

She nodded, and he walked away with long, determined strides. She only hoped he was right. That nothing interrupted their dinner tomorrow.

CHAPTER 14

Cassie knocked on the door to the owner's suite at The Cabot at precisely six o'clock the next evening. This time she'd only tried on *two* outfits before deciding what to wear. Simple navy slacks and a knit top with narrow navy stripes. She thought it looked rather nautical and fitting for a date at a hotel on the harbor.

The door swung open and Del stood there with a dish towel tossed over one shoulder and his hair slightly mussed. "Come in." His welcoming smile warmed her as he reached out and took her hand.

"Something smells wonderful."

"It's a chicken dish. Hope you like it. I'm not

the best cook, but I can follow a recipe." He grinned.

She stepped into the suite that used to be her home, feeling a bit out of place and caught between two worlds. She'd lived here for so many years with her parents, then just her father. And now it was Del's home.

"You okay?" He looked at her closely.

"I am… just… memories again." She scanned the room. "I love that the walls are a lighter color now. Really brightens the room." She followed him toward the kitchen and gasped when she entered. "Wow… this is… wonderful." Shiny stainless appliances were tucked into muted gray stained cabinets. The counters were redone in a light grayish granite, and lights flooded the room.

"I did have a lot of work done in here. There were still some old copper-toned appliances in here. The stove didn't work. Damage to the cabinetry. So I had it gutted and redone."

"It's wonderful."

"Not too hard to see it all changed from when you lived here?"

"No, not really." Well, it kind of was, but she didn't want to dwell on it.

He laughed. "You're just partially telling the truth. I can still read your expressions."

She blushed. "Okay, it's a bit difficult to see it so different. But it really is lovely."

He smiled at her. That smile of his that made her lose her train of thought.

"Dinner will be ready in a bit. Would you like to go out and sit on the patio?"

What had he said? Oh, the patio. "Yes, that sounds nice."

They headed outside with glasses of wine. Delbert had lined two sides of the patio with hedges to afford some privacy and added a slatted pergola above. Wicker furniture with plump striped cushions beckoned, with a beautiful view of the bay. They settled onto a loveseat, and the warmth of his body spread through her. But she ignored it, of course. She was having a hard enough time with his smile— she didn't need to concentrate on how close he was sitting.

"I was worried that all the changes might bother you." He didn't look like sitting so close to her bothered him one bit.

"Honestly? Our living quarters were so run down by the time we left. Father didn't want to spend any money on them when the hotel needed so much work." She glanced out toward the bay, watching a pair of seagulls swoop by. "And I have wonderful memories of it, too. We were really happy here when I was young. Then Uncle Ted left, mother passed away, and the bills kept piling up. Then all that damage from the hurricane. It was too much for Father." She turned back to him. "I'm glad you brightened the place up and made it your own. I hope it feels like home to you now."

"It does. I rather enjoy being able to head down the hall to the owner's suite at the end of the day. I made an office out of one of the extra bedrooms. Sometimes I like to hide out in there instead of my official office in the hotel." An easy smiled played at the corner of his lips. Not that she was looking at his lips. "And there is another bedroom—painted teal—was that yours?"

She laughed. "It was. I went through a teal period in my life. Teal everything. My father did let me paint my room teal."

"It certainly is… bright." He grinned at her. "But, for now, I'm leaving it alone. I don't really need this many bedrooms, but that's what the suite has, so I guess three bedrooms it is."

She cleared her throat. "So, you're planning on staying here for a while? Running your business from here?"

"That's the plan. I've hired a new acquisitions manager to do some of the traveling I used to do. I'm a bit tired of traveling all over all the time. I actually really like running The Cabot. Usually I negotiate to buy a hotel. Coordinate some of the remodeling. Come for the reopening, then pop in once a year or so to check on things. It's been nice to stick around and watch The Cabot reopening and things get smoothed out." He shrugged. "I can run a lot of the Hamilton Hotels business from here. It's amazing what you can get done working remotely these days."

"You're right about that. I had an online meeting today... from the balcony of my suite. Problems with a fundraiser we're having, but we got it all sorted out."

"The marvels of modern technology." As if on cue, his phone pinged. "Ah, but then there are the downsides."

She held her breath, wondering if their plans would be cut short yet again.

"I'm going to put this phone on silent.

There's nothing that needs to be dealt with tonight."

"Unless there's another emergency." She eyed him. Would he really turn off his phone for her?

Impressive. He did switch the phone to silent.

"I'm sure they'd come knocking on my door if that happens. But I warned the night manager that short of a hurricane, a fire, or similar disaster, that I was off tonight." He took her hand in his. "I've waited a long time for this night."

She glanced down at their intertwined fingers. "I have, too. All those years ago, I thought that you'd finally ask me out the next time you visited."

"But I didn't come back, did I?"

"No, and I really missed you that summer."

He squeezed her hand. "I know. I missed you, too. It didn't feel like summer without my visit to Moonbeam. I even checked into getting a bus ticket to come here by myself, but my mother squashed that idea."

"You did?"

"Of course. I could hardly bear thinking about not seeing you. Coming here was the highlight of every summer." He locked his eyes with hers. "The highlight of every *year*."

He reached over and brushed a lock of curls from her cheek, trailing his finger along her jaw. She swallowed, unable to break free of his probing look.

He suddenly stood and pulled her to her feet. Still looking at her intently, he placed two fingers under her chin and tilted her face up. Then... as if in slow motion... he lowered his lips to hers.

Finally.

After all these years.

The connection and emotion his kiss brought made her reach out both hands to cling to his arms. He deepened the kiss, and she couldn't help the sigh that escaped. He finally pulled away and gave a little laugh, running his hand through his hair. "Ah... I've waited a long time for that."

She stood there mutely, barely able to collect her thoughts, still clinging to his arms.

"I think I'd like to try that again." He cocked his head to the side with an impish grin on his lips.

She nodded and waited.

He wrapped his arms around her and pulled

her close. Close enough that she could feel his heartbeat. Then he kissed her again, and the world faded away. It was just the two of them. No one else. The years they'd been apart evaporated into the evening air.

He finally broke off the kiss, a bemused expression on his face. "That was... nice."

She just nodded.

"Are you ever going to speak to me again?" He reached out and touched her lips.

"I—" She took in a deep breath. "I will if you can stop kissing me long enough for me to gather my wits about me."

"Wits are overrated." He leaned in and kissed her again.

She wasn't sure how long they stood there kissing and holding each other. Long enough that the first stars came out, and the sun began to dip below the horizon.

He finally laughed and pulled away. "I'm going to go rescue our dinner if I can. I think it was ready quite a while ago." He led her inside and pulled the chicken out of the oven. The severely over-baked chicken. Burnt even. He shook his head as he set it on the stovetop. "Well, that's not good. I ruined dinner." He winked at her. "But it was worth it. I'd rather starve than give up kissing you."

She laughed. "Open up your cabinets and let's see what we can throw together."

"Really? You're one of those cooks who can make a meal out of nothing?" He eyed her with a hopeful glint in his eyes.

"Not out of nothing, but let's look and see what you have."

She found pasta in the cupboard and bacon in the fridge, so she made pasta carbonara. His frozen green beans became green bean almondine. Luckily he'd made a salad, so they added that to their meal.

They sat out on the patio eating their put-together meal and sipping wine. A quartet of lanterns in the corners of the patio illuminated the area with warm, magical light. The breeze picked up, and she shivered slightly.

"Are you chilly? We could move inside."

"No, I'm okay." She didn't really want to leave the pretty patio and the view.

"How about I go in and grab you a sweater?" He went inside and returned with a sweater and slipped it over her head. As it settled on her, she basked in the feeling of having him surround her.

"Thank you." She rolled up the sleeves a bit. They finished their meal, then sat for a bit, sipping their wine.

They finally carried the dishes inside, and she helped him clean up. Then they stood in the kitchen, staring at each other, grinning like fools.

Happy fools.

"You want to go back out to the patio and neck?" He winked.

"Mr. Hamilton. How forward you are," she teased.

"I guess we could end the evening." He settled a forlorn look on his face, though his eyes twinkled.

She pulled him close. "I'm not ready for it to end." She stood on tiptoe and kissed him.

He took her hand and led her outside again. They sat close together, talking, laughing, and kissing far into the late hours of the night. He finally walked her back to her suite, kissing her once in the doorway before leaving. She closed the door behind her, pressing two fingers to her lips, still warm from his kiss.

She hugged herself, still surrounded by his sweater. She bunched it up in the front and sank her face in it. It smelled like Del. Clean, woodsy, male.

She went over to the window without turning on a light and looked out over the bay. This was a night she'd remember forever. Her first kiss from Delbert Hamilton—and many more kisses after that first one.

CHAPTER 15

"Aw, do you have to go?" Austin tugged at Olivia's hand. "I thought you were taking some time off."

"I have taken time off." She shrugged. "I'm not very good at just sitting around."

Austin cocked his head and gave her a mischievous grin. "So *that's* what you call it? Sitting around?"

She blushed. "You know what I mean. I just... want to check on things at Sea Glass Cafe. See if Evelyn needs any help. She'd done so much the last few weeks while we planned the wedding, and now this week, too."

"It's Wednesday. We've only been married for four days." He tugged her into his lap and wrapped his arms around her. "Can't I convince you to stay?"

"I really should go."

He kissed her.

"Really, Austin. I have responsibilities."

"Uh-huh." He nodded in agreement and kissed her again.

She sighed. "You don't make it very easy, do you?"

"I'm not trying to make it easy." His lips curled into a confident smile.

Her phone dinged, and she reached for it and read the text. "Oh, it's Emily. She's home from school and wants to know when I'm coming home. I'd told her sometime this week. I think... I think maybe I should go back today?"

Austin let out a long sigh. "It seems like our stay-at-home honeymoon is coming to an end."

"And we still haven't decided on the whole living situation. I can't believe we didn't sort it out before the wedding." She shook her head.

"Well, we were a little rushed moving it up so quickly." He pushed her hair away from her face. "What do you want to do? Where do you want us to live?"

"I do like my house. Living on the canal. Boating over to Mom's. But my house is really small." She climbed off his lap and walked over to the window. "And I do love having the view of the beach like you do here, but you're renting. So if Emily and I moved here, we'd have to eventually move again."

"So what if we look for a new house to buy? One on the beach?"

"Can we afford that?" She frowned. "We haven't really talked about money, either, have we? The things most couples discuss before the wedding. Where they're going to live. Finances."

"We'll work all that out. I promise." He got up and walked over to stand beside her. "How about we pack up some of my things, and we'll head back to your house? Emily is comfortable there, it's the home she knows. We'll be fine there for a bit. Then all three of us will start looking for a home, as long as Emily is okay with moving."

"I think she'll be fine with it."

"Then text her back that we're heading over and we'll sit down and talk to her. Unless you want to talk to her alone?"

"No, let's both talk to her." She gave him a smile. "And you think we could take a quick stop by the cafe after that?"

He laughed, grabbed both her hands, and

tugged her close. "Yes, we'll go to the cafe, too. I'd do anything to keep my bride happy."

They headed back to her house with a suitcase of Austin's things. She pushed through the front door. "Emily?"

Emily came walking out from the kitchen. "Ah, it's the happy married couple."

Olivia gave Emily a hug. "Missed you."

"Mom, it's been like a couple days." She shook her head. "I just made some tea. You guys want some?"

They headed to the kitchen and settled around the small table. Emily leaned back in her chair. "So, Austin. You're not going to hog all the hot water in the mornings for your shower, are you?" Emily grinned.

He laughed. "Nah, I'm a quick shower guy."

"Good, because usually Mom and I fight each other over the last drops of hot water."

"Em, we were thinking… this house is kind of small for all three of us." She looked at Emily carefully, judging her reaction.

Emily looked over at her and frowned. "So you want me to move out?"

"What, no!" Her eyes widened. "Of course not."

Emily laughed. "Mom, I was just teasing."

Relief swept through her. "Oh... of course. I knew that."

Emily rolled her eyes.

"Your mother and I were thinking about looking for a little bit bigger house. Maybe on the beach on the gulf or the harbor?"

"I'm good with that."

Olivia reached out and took Emily's hand. "You're sure you're okay with moving?"

"Mom, I'm leaving for college soon, anyway. So wherever you guys want to live is fine with me. It will be kind of fun to go house hunting."

"It will, won't it?" She smiled at her daughter, grateful for her willing attitude. She turned to Austin. "Now can we go check in at the cafe?"

"Mom, you're supposed to be off this week." Emily shook her head.

"But I want to make sure everything is okay."

Emily laughed. "Evelyn said you wouldn't make it all week without going in. She was right."

Olivia stood. "Well then, I'm only going in so that Evelyn was right about me."

Austin stood. "Come, Liv. I'll walk you over.

Then I think I'll treat myself to some ice cream."

She turned to Emily. "So, dinner here tonight? The three of us?"

"Sounds great. I'm headed to the beach with Blake and Angela and some friends. I'll be back by dinner."

"Okay. See you then." She and Austin headed out the door. Pausing at the bottom of the steps, she turned to him. "You know what? We're going to have our first family dinner tonight."

"One of many." He kissed her gently. "So, what are we having?"

"We'll have to pick up something on the way home. Maybe barbecue some steaks and a big salad?"

"And maybe some of Evelyn's pie for dessert?"

"Sounds like a plan." She slipped her hand in Austin's and they headed down the sidewalk, side by side. A married couple planning what's for dinner. She still couldn't quite wrap her mind around that fact.

Donna looked up and laughed when she saw Livy and Austin walking into Parker's. "Well, that honeymoon didn't last long."

"I just thought I should come check on things." Olivia laughed. "And Austin was a good sport about it."

"What she means is I was promised some ice cream." He grinned and looked at Olivia with adoring eyes. "Plus anything that makes Livy happy, makes me happy."

She smiled at the two of them, obviously so in love. What more could a mother hope for her daughter?

"I really tried to stay away. But Evelyn did so much while we were planning the wedding. And I know she has that charity event at the hotel on Friday. I just..."

Donna laughed. "I'm not blaming you. Parker's gets in your blood. It becomes part of you."

"It does." Olivia nodded.

The door opened behind them, and Donna steeled herself when she saw it was Charlie. She'd clung to the faint hope that maybe he'd left town, but that hope was shattered now.

"I thought I saw my girl come in here to Parker's." Charlie walked up to them.

"Hi, Charlie. I didn't know you were still in town." Olivia glanced at Donna.

Donna shook her head in reply. "What are you doing still here, Charlie?" Ouch, that probably was a little too blunt. But really, the man had walked out on her, on Olivia. How civil was she supposed to be?

"Just wanted to stick around and see if I could have some more time with my girl."

"She's on her honeymoon, Charlie. I don't think she has time for that right now."

"And yet, here she is at Parker's."

"I'm just here for a quick check on things, then Austin and I are headed back home."

"Mind my words, son. Parker's will always come first with these women, not you."

"I don't mind. I love that Livy enjoys working at the cafe so much. I admire all she's done to make it a success."

Olivia frowned. "And Charlie, that's not true. Emily has always come first for me. And now Austin, too."

"I sure wasn't high on your mother's list when I was married to her. Parker's always came first."

"Maybe because I was trying to support all of us while raising our daughter." Donna hadn't meant to say that out loud, but Charlie had a way of getting under her skin. And he'd given up any right to comment on her life when he walked out of it so many years ago. Anger simmered just barely under the surface.

"Whatever. Maybe I would have stuck around longer if you'd acted like I was wanted around here."

She stood in stunned silence. She'd tried everything to make their marriage work. Suggested counseling. Supported him when he popped from job to job, only to quit each one. Put up with his late nights out drinking with the boys. His spending money they didn't really have. So what? Now it was her fault he left when things got tough? She glanced at Olivia. Did *Olivia* blame her for Charlie leaving?

Olivia stepped up to him, her eyes flashing. "Mom's not to blame for you leaving. It was your choice. It was also your choice to not come and see me very often. You go years and years without visiting. That's not Mom's fault either. That's on you."

"Why is it always a drama with you Parker women? See, I can't ever do anything right. Say anything right." Charlie shook his head in disgust.

"And don't you put the blame on Olivia, either." Donna walked over and put an arm around Olivia's shoulders.

"Right, everything is my fault. Always was. Always will be." Charlie held up his hands. "I give up on you Parker women." He turned and stalked out of the store.

"He gave up on us a long time ago," Olivia said softly. "But you were always there for me, Mom. Always."

"And I always will be." She hugged her daughter. "I'm sorry Charlie can be so difficult."

"Even though he thinks it's us being difficult?"

"Even though. Charlie never was one to take responsibility for his actions or his words... or for anything."

"Do you think he'll leave town now?"

"I have no idea. I long ago quit guessing what Charlie was going to do." Donna shrugged. "Why don't you go get Austin that ice cream?"

"Mom is right. Let's get ice cream." Olivia took Austin's hand, and they headed into the cafe.

Donna stood staring at the door that Charlie had just stormed out of and let out a long breath. The man still had a way of getting her all off-kilter. She really had tried everything to make their marriage work. She had. But Charlie would never see it that way. Would never take responsibility for any mistakes. Any of his choices. A different woman might have dragged him through court, demanding child support, but she didn't have the time or energy. And besides the anger that he just up and left, she'd felt a bit of relief. At least she didn't have to cover his spending and put up with his criticism and the constant arguing.

She shook her head, hoping that Charlie would leave town now. She was tired of his remarks. And even though he'd left, even though he rarely, if ever, sent anything to Olivia or helped support her, she'd never done a thing to keep him from having a relationship with her, if he'd wanted it. And yet... he'd never really tried.

Barry walked in the front door. "Was that Charlie I saw leaving?"

She sighed. "It was."

"You okay?"

"I will be. He just... gets under my skin. I need to learn to not let him get to me."

Barry kissed her gently. "I could go have a man-to-man talk with him, you know."

"No, Charlie is my problem." She smiled up at him. "And with any luck, he'll leave now. Which probably means we have another ten years before we have to deal with him again."

CHAPTER 16

Delbert looked up from his desk in his office to see Cassandra standing in the doorway. A smile spread across his face as he jumped to his feet. "Cassandra, hello. Come in."

He crossed the floor and took her hand, pulling her into the office and closing the door behind her. Then he stopped, trying to decide if he should kiss her or not. They'd had plenty of kisses last night, but in the light of day... would she still want a kiss? Were they at the kiss hello stage?

She stood on tiptoe, balancing herself by placing her hands on his shoulders, and kissed him gently.

That answered that question.

Yes, they were at the kiss hello stage.

She stepped back. "I woke up this morning and kissing you was the first thing on my mind." She grinned. "But I had an online meeting or two. But once they were finished, I came to find you."

"And I'm glad you found me." He tugged on her hand and pulled her close, running his hand through her hair, marveling at how perfect she felt in his arms. "What are your plans for the rest of the day?" he asked but didn't let her go.

"I have another meeting soon. Online. Then I'd planned for a beach walk. Do you think you could slip away for a bit late afternoon?"

"Ah, I have a meeting that will probably last all afternoon. We're having a big event on Friday. This is the final meeting about it. Usually Evelyn does all of this, but she's busy at the cafe with Livy on her honeymoon. I told her I would handle it." Disappointment flashed through him. "But how about dinner tonight?"

"Oh, I told Uncle Ted that I'd have dinner at his place tonight."

Del sighed. "Looks like our schedules are a bit off, doesn't it?"

"I could meet you for a nightcap tonight? Out on the porch?"

"That would work." Though he wouldn't be able to kiss her over and over like he had last night. That was a bit of a disappointment.

"Perfect. Say about eight-thirty or so? I can text you when I'm leaving Uncle Ted's."

"Great." He leaned down and kissed her again. Then once more to tide him over until this evening.

She grinned as she pulled away and headed for the door. "I'll be looking for another of those when I see you tonight."

He shook his head. He should have suggested that she come to his apartment for the nightcap. Then they could have had unlimited kisses far away from any prying eyes.

That evening, Cassandra walked out onto the porch of The Cabot, looking for Del. He waved to her from a pair of chairs at the far end of the porch. She hurried over and sat down beside him.

He leaned over the table between them and

kissed her quickly, then smiled as he settled back in his chair. "I went ahead and grabbed a bottle of wine. Is that okay?"

She glanced at the bottle and saw that he'd picked one of her favorite cabernets. "Yes, that's wonderful."

He poured them each a glass and handed one to her. They briefly clinked glasses, and she took a sip of the rich, mahogany-colored wine. "Oh, this is so good."

"Glad you like it."

"How do you remember so many of the little details? Like my favorite wine. Favorite flower."

He shrugged. "Those details are important to me."

Her heart warmed with his answers. She loved the fact that details about her were important to him. She hadn't had that with Vincent. She doubted he knew her favorite color, favorite flower… and yet she'd dated him for years. She pushed the thought of him far away.

She reached over and took Del's hand. They sat in silence for a bit, sipping their wine and looking out over the moonlight on the harbor.

"So, how was your dinner with Ted?"

"Wonderful, as always. He's the best chef."

"So he didn't ruin his dinner like I did?" He sent her a rueful look.

"You didn't ruin it." She laughed gently. "Well, you kind of did. But we ended up with a nice meal anyway, didn't we?"

"And if I have to ruin a meal, kissing you is as good a reason for ruining it as any."

A slight blush crept across her face as she remembered their many, many kisses. She pushed the thought away. "And how was your meeting about the event?"

"It went well. Though I freely admit I prefer when Evelyn takes care of all of this."

"What is the event?"

"It's a charity event for the history museum." He looked at her. "I was wondering. I mean, would you like to go with me? Come to the event? I think it will be very nice. Evelyn has helped with a lot of the arrangements and planning the food. Donna and Barry are on the guest list. I think I saw Ted on it, too, so he'll probably be there with Patricia. It's a fancy deal, though. Black tie. Gowns."

"Oh, I didn't bring anything appropriate to wear." She was kind of disappointed. The event did sound like fun.

"Oh." He looked crestfallen.

She looked over at him, and her lips curled into a tiny smile. "But... I suppose I could do a bit of shopping tomorrow."

His face lit up with excitement. "You could? That would be great."

"Yes, I'll find something. It does sound like fun."

"Perfect." He clinked his glass to hers again. "To yet another date."

"Another date." She took a sip of her wine, watching his face over the rim of her glass. Seeing his eyes glow with anticipation.

"And how about tomorrow? We don't want to let tomorrow slip by without doing something together, do we?" He looked at her expectantly.

"No, I don't suppose we do."

"Late afternoon harbor walk? Then dinner at my place again? I think I'll have the chef make something, though. Something I can just keep warm in the oven." A glimmer of humor flickered in his features.

"Yes, that would be lovely." She wasn't ready to let a day go by without seeing him on her short trip to town, either. Not after they'd reconnected. Not after he'd kissed her. Not after she'd slowly unwrapped her long-hidden feelings for him.

"Great." He sent her a smile that made her pulse race.

Alone again with Delbert. And maybe some more time for his kisses. Lots of his kisses.

CHAPTER 17

The next afternoon Cassandra met Delbert at the owner's suite, and they headed out for a walk along the harbor. They walked and chatted and pointed out things to each other. Sailboats that slipped past under motor, heading out to the deeper part of the harbor to unfurl their sails. A large yacht with music blaring and people spilling onto all levels of the boat. A lone fisherman bobbing in his small fishing boat just offshore. A lone blue heron wading at the waters' edge. Everything seemed special and new when shared with Del.

The wind picked up and whipped around them. Her hair flew in all directions and she wished she would have thought to have pulled it back. She gathered the curls in one hand as they walked along.

"Sure is breezy today, isn't it? I heard a storm is headed in this evening." Delbert glanced up at the sky. "It looks like it's darkening a bit in that direction."

She glanced in the direction he pointed. Clouds of dark blue and grey gathered. "Does look like a storm is headed for us."

They walked a bit further, then Del paused, looking at the sky again. "Maybe we should head back. It looks like it's coming in faster than I thought."

She nodded, and they turned around. Soon they picked up their pace as the storm got closer. Finally, before they could reach the safety of the hotel, large raindrops splattered around them. Delbert grabbed her hand. "Let's make a run for it."

They raced, hand in hand, along the end of the harbor walk and cut up toward the hotel. But not before they were soaked to the skin. They reached Delbert's suite, and he opened the door for her to slip inside. She stood dripping on the rug by the door.

"Let me get us some towels." Delbert

disappeared and returned with big, thirsty towels.

She dried off as best she could, shivering slightly. "I should head up to my room and change clothes."

"That's probably a good idea. I'll change into dry clothes, too."

"I'll be back soon." She slipped out of his suite and headed to her room.

She went into her room and looked in the mirror. She looked like a bedraggled kitten and was sorry Del had seen her looking like that. Slipping off her wet clothes, she headed to the bathroom and hung them to drip dry in the shower. She dried off yet again and went to her closet, picking out a pair of slacks, a knit top, and a teal sweater. She debated drying her hair and curling it with the flat iron... but her hair was thick and it would take a long time. Way too much time. She finger brushed the curls and left them to dry on their own. A quick re-touch of makeup, and she was ready to head back to Del's.

When she returned, he'd changed into slacks and a knit shirt. His hair was still damp. "I heated some water. Would you like some hot tea to warm you up?"

"Yes, that sounds wonderful."

They made their tea in big mugs and carried it over to a pair of chairs by the window. Lightning flashed in the sky and rain poured down, slashing through the slats on the pergola and dancing around on the patio.

"That wasn't exactly in my plans for a leisurely walk with you." Del smiled and took a sip of his tea.

"Nor mine." She laughed. "But do you remember that time that one summer when we got caught in the storm out on the beach? We hid out under the porch of that deserted beach house?"

"I remember that. It was the last summer I came here." A thoughtful look crossed his features. "I remember wondering if I should kiss you. But I never got up the nerve."

"You were going to kiss me?"

"Sure was. Only… I chickened out."

"That's too bad… I would have liked that."

"At least I can kiss you whenever I want now." He grinned and leaned over and kissed her.

She laughed. "Yes. Yes, you can."

"I wonder if things would have been

different if I had kissed you back then." A crease furrowed his brow. "Would we have tried harder to keep in touch? Maybe all these years wouldn't have slipped by without seeing each other."

She looked out at a flash of lightning, then back at Del. "I guess we'll never know."

"I regret that choice. Not kissing you then."

"We all have choices in life we regret. But we can't change them later. We don't get a do-over."

"But we kind of did. Didn't we? This chance again?" He reached over and touched her face. "And I'm so grateful for it."

"I am, too."

"And not taking that chance all those years ago. It taught me something."

"What's that?"

"Never let the opportunity pass by to do what feels right." He took one of her hands in his, holding it tightly. "So... I'm going to take a chance and tell you something."

She held her breath, her eyes locked with his.

"Cassandra... I love you. I have since I was a boy. It's never wavered. I know we've just started dating, but it doesn't change how I feel. And I want to make sure you know how I feel about you."

"You... what did you say?" Her pulse pounded in her ears, and she wasn't sure she'd heard him correctly. Had he really said what she'd wanted to hear for all these years?

"I said that I love you."

She swallowed, her heart pounding. "Delbert... I feel the same way. I've felt this way my whole life, it seems. That first summer when we were just kids, and we spent hours together. Exploring the beaches. Collecting shells. And talking. Always talking. Then as we got older... I figured out it was more than friendship. How deeply I cared about you."

He looked at her, his eyes filled with warmth and emotion.

She waited for the words to form. The ones she'd wanted to say to him for so very many years. "I love you, Delbert Hamilton. With every fiber in my being. With my whole heart."

He leaned over and kissed her. "That, I think, is the most wonderful thing I've ever heard."

Cassandra stood out on the balcony of the Bay Suite long after Delbert had walked her back to her room. She didn't want the day to end. She took out each minute of the evening and examined it like a person would do when they found a stack of long-lost photographs. Remembering every little detail, every feeling.

Delbert Hamilton loved her.

Her heart filled at the thought. And she truly loved him. She had for years. The men she'd dated had always fallen short compared to Del.

Especially Vincent, the cheater.

Though there was a small part of her she held back, even from Del. She wanted to believe his feelings for her, and she did. As much as she could. Del was different than Vincent. Kinder. An honest man.

But then, she'd thought she really knew Vincent, too. She'd been sure they were going to get married.

Until he proved her wrong. So very wrong.

She got up and walked back inside, closing the door behind her. It might take some time, but she was sure that after a while she'd get over the distrust that Vincent had so firmly etched in her very soul.

And Del would be just the man to help her get over it. She smiled to herself as she went to get ready for bed.

Delbert Hamilton loved her.

CHAPTER 18

Violet headed into Parker's General Store on Friday morning. She'd announced to her guests that she was going to have Friday evening happy hour. Then she realized she had nothing to ice up soda and beer in except for the old, stained cooler she'd been so embarrassed by at Livy and Austin's rehearsal. Time for something new.

She approached Melody Tanner working at the front counter. She'd met her a few times when she'd come into the store or the cafe.

"Violet, hi." Melody turned from where she was stacking some items on shelves behind the counter.

"Hi, Melody. I'm going to start having a Friday happy hour at the Blue Heron, but my cooler is way past its prime. Do you have something I could use to ice up some drinks?"

"We do have some coolers." Melody's brow creased. "But you know what? We have some new galvanized wash tubs that would be really cute to use."

"Oh, I like that idea." Her mind started spinning. The washtub of drinks. Maybe a galvanized watering can planted with fresh flowers? It sounded cute and homey.

"It's upstairs in the new seasonal room. There are also lots of beachy decor items up there. Cute trays. Napkins. Things like that."

"Oh, I'll go look up there." She climbed the stairs and browsed around for a bit before coming back downstairs with the washtub full of other items she'd found. A cute tray painted with seashells. A wooden napkin holder along with some adorable beach-themed napkins.

"Looks like you found all you need." Melody nodded toward the pile of items she dumped on the counter.

"I'm still hoping to find a watering can to use as a planter."

"Oh, those are in the back corner. Come, I'll show you."

She followed Melody to the back of the

store, where there was a collection of watering cans. Galvanized steel, or a cute, bright-yellow metal one. She chewed her lip, trying to decide.

"I'd go with the yellow one. You have such nice bright cottages at the Blue Heron. It will fit in nicely."

She laughed. "Thank you. I feel like I've made so many decisions about so many things in the last few months. I'm about decisioned out."

Melody rang up her order, and a man came into the store. "Hi, Ethan," Melody called out.

She turned to look at the tall, thin man who she swore blushed slightly at Melody's greeting.

"Come over for a sec." Melody waved to the man. "Have you met Violet? She's the one who took over Murphy's and turned it into Blue Heron Cottages."

The man walked over and gave her an awkward smile. "Nice to meet you, ma'am." His voice was low and soft-spoken. "I'm Ethan Chambers."

"Hi, Ethan. Nice to meet you."

Ethan nodded, then darted a glance at Melody. She sensed something going on there. At least on Ethan's part. Melody seemed totally clueless.

"I should get going. I'll drop these in my car, then I have some appetizers to pick up at the cafe. Oh, and ice. I can't forget the ice." She turned to Melody. "Thanks so much for your help. You should stop by the cottages some Friday for our happy hour. I'd love to have you join us."

She turned to Ethan. "You, too. Love to have you. It's just simple. Beer, soda, wine. A few snacks."

"I appreciate the offer. I just might do that." Ethan bobbed his head, then snuck another look at Melody.

"Maybe you two could find a Friday to come together. I'd really love to have you." With that, she scooped up her purchases and headed out to the car, hoping her little push might convince Ethan to suggest to Melody that they come to her happy hour. She'd love to get to know more of the townsfolk, and they seemed like a good place to start. Of course, she knew Evelyn and her family because of Rob. But she wouldn't mind having more friends in town. Well, *any* friends in town. She'd been so busy getting the cottages ready, she hadn't really had time to make friends. But now Moonbeam was her home. It was time to get to know more of the locals.

Now if Ethan would take her hint and ask Melody to come to a happy hour, she could get started on her making-friends plan.

CHAPTER 19

Cassandra spread out the gown she'd found at Barbara's Boutique here in town. The owner, Margaret, had helped her pick it out. A simple emerald green, full-length dress that looked like it had been made for her. She'd been surprised with the selection at the boutique and assured Margaret she'd be back in again soon.

Some simple silver heels, not too high, but very cute, finished the outfit.

She carefully pulled her hair up into a twisted knot, with curls falling to frame her face. She put on a bit more makeup than normal, but still not too much. Then a touch of lipstick to top it off.

She stood in front of the full-length mirror affixed to the back of the bathroom door, turning this way and that, pleased with how the outfit, her hair, her makeup… everything looked perfect. There was something special about getting all dressed up for an event.

A memory flashed through her mind of the first fancy event she could remember going to at The Cabot. She'd been a young girl and she and her mother wore matching red and green dresses for a big Christmas party in the ballroom. Her shoes were red with sparkles on them. She remembered those shoes vividly. An enormous tree had been decorated at the end of the ballroom with sparkling lights and what seemed like a million silver balls. The windows had been draped in greenery and the heady scent of evergreen swirled through the room. She'd felt like a princess that night. Her father and her uncle took turns dancing with her out on the dance floor, and her mother had let her stay up way past her bedtime.

She clung to the precious memory for a few more moments before letting it slip away. Things were different now, but once again she was headed to a big, fancy event at The Cabot.

"I love seeing the hotel full of people again. So alive."

"Barry helped with the remodel, did you know that?"

"Del told me that. Barry, it really turned out so nice. Very close to how it was when my family owned it, but updated and sparkly. It's just lovely."

"That's what we were shooting for." Barry beamed at the compliment.

"Well, Donna, *Barney*, fancy meeting you here."

Donna stiffened at the sound of Charlie's voice. Her mouth dropped open before she could catch herself, and she slowly turned around to face him. She didn't even bother to correct him. She was certain he knew Barry's name.

And to add to her shock, Camille Montgomery was hanging onto his arm. How did that happen? How in the world did they know each other?

"And I assume you know Camille?" Charlie's lips widened into a grin that bordered on a smirk.

"Yes, hello, Camille." Not that she was happy to see her. She still hadn't forgiven the woman for being so rude to Emily when she was working on the history alcove for the hotel, but she put on a polite smile. It was getting to be a habit around Charlie.

"Camille, Donna here is my ex-wife."

"Really?" Camille's eyes widened. "I didn't know that."

"Now you do." Charlie bobbed his head. "But, now she's married to Barney."

Barry looked at her questioningly, and she shook her head ever so slightly.

"Oh, and you're that Cabot woman, aren't you?" Camille looked carefully at Cassandra with an obvious, appraising gaze.

"Yes, this is Cassandra Cabot," Donna confirmed.

"Nice to see you again, Camille," Cassandra said politely.

So much politeness swirling around, and all she could think of was finding a way to escape it.

"I met Camille at a party this week. She was with some boring banker guy." He turned to Camille. "Sorry, hon, but it's the truth. I'm a much better date."

Camille laughed. "You are. I was getting tired

of him, anyway. I swear, he always ended our dates by nine o'clock. But that's when most events just really start to get going. What a stick in the mud."

"Well, I'm a stay out late and party guy, so you're in luck." Charlie flashed the gregarious smile that he thought was so charming.

Donna didn't find it charming at all. She knew it was fake, but obviously, Camille didn't. It looked like Camille had fallen for his charms. And Charlie could be ever so charming when he wanted to be. Especially when there was something in it for him.

Camille always seemed to date the rich, influential men since her breakup with Delbert. Maybe she hadn't quite figured out Charlie was all talk. Smoke and mirrors. Acted rich, but rarely had any money to his name.

But then, Camille wasn't her problem. She'd find out soon enough.

"So, you and old Barney here. Didn't know you ran with the movers and shakers in town. Didn't expect to see you here at this shindig."

"You know perfectly well that his name is Barry." She couldn't help herself.

"Right, Barry." Charlie grinned and winked. "Barry. I'll remember that."

"So, how long do you plan on staying in town, Charlie?" Barry asked.

"Why? Does it bother you having Donna's ex in town?"

"Not at all," Barry said politely. There was that politeness again. But she could tell by the set of his shoulders that he was about as fed up with Charlie as she was. "Donna, how about that dance you promised me?" Barry threw her a lifeline.

"Yes, let's." She turned to Cassandra, intent on saving her, too. "Cassandra? You coming inside? I think I saw Ted and Mom walk past."

"Yes, I do want to go find Uncle Ted." Cassandra smiled—politely—at Camille. "Nice to see you again."

Barry took her hand, and they started to head back inside the ballroom. At this point, she didn't even mind the crowd or the noise. Much more preferable than being out on the patio with Charlie.

"Don't keep her out too late, Barney. She's not a late-night type of gal," Charlie called after them.

Donna gritted her teeth and refused to turn around.

"Don't pay any attention to him," Barry

whispered. "He's just jealous that I have the most beautiful woman in the room on my arm."

She gave him a grateful look, and they walked inside. Soon they were—*thankfully*—swallowed by the crowd.

CHAPTER 20

Cassandra stepped into the ladies' room, as much for a break from the crowds as anything. She hadn't located Delbert again. He was probably busy with something important. But she was tiring of the event and would love to find him and escape to the porch or the gardens for some time alone together like he'd suggested.

Camille stood at the counter, freshening her makeup.

"Hello, Camille."

"Hello," the woman said as she applied a layer of bright red lipstick, pressed her lips together, and turned to her, smiling. "A woman needs to keep her makeup looking fresh, doesn't she?"

Cassandra hadn't really planned on touching up her makeup, but maybe she should? She took a look in the mirror. She thought she still looked okay?

Camille put the lipstick in her purse. "Did you come to the event alone?"

"I… ah, I'm here with Delbert Hamilton."

"I heard that you and Delbert seem to be getting close." The woman frowned slightly. "Hmm…"

What did that hmm mean?

"I… We…" She didn't know how to answer. "We're friends." She'd leave it at that.

"Ah, friends." Camille smiled knowingly. "Delbert and his *friends*."

She didn't like the way Camille said the word friends…

"Delbert and I dated for years, did he tell you that?" Camille cocked her head, with one eyebrow slightly raised.

"No, I didn't know that." But, of course, Delbert dated before. So had she. And Camille was a beautiful woman.

"We dated for a *very* long time. He loved me." Camille gave a delicate shrug. "But then… well…" Camille lowered her voice. "I found out he cheated on me. The woman is always the last to know, isn't she? Delbert seems like the perfect gentleman. Always. Everyone adores him. Everyone thinks he's the best. I think that's why he hid his affairs from me. *Multiple* affairs. And I had no clue. Even when he was professing his love for me."

She stared at Camille, open mouthed. *What* was Camille saying to her?

"When I found out, I, of course, broke up with him. He begged me to take him back, but I said no. Men don't cheat on Camille Montgomery. I will not let them make a fool out of me."

"He cheated?" Her voice cracked and the words slipped out. She hadn't meant to say them.

"He did. And I was a fool not to pick up on it. I should have known."

Just like she should have known when Vincent cheated on her. She knew the horrible feeling when the truth came out. Suddenly she felt a close affinity to Camille. Knew exactly what she'd gone through.

"Anyway, if you and Delbert are getting close, becoming an item... well... I just thought you should know what kind of man he really is, no matter how endearing he might seem."

Cassandra's thoughts bounced around the room, her mind reeling. Was Delbert just like Vincent? Look at Camille. She was beautiful. Charming, even. And kind enough to tell her the truth about Delbert.

Was he hiding the same thing from her? Seeing someone else while professing his love for her? Who was that woman in the shimmering black gown he'd been talking to tonight? Their heads had been close, talking intently. And where had he disappeared to? She hadn't been able to find him for over an hour.

Was Delbert really just a cheater who hid it well? Or, when the newness of their relationship wore off... is that when he'd find someone else? Would he hide it from her, too, like he did with Camille?

Disappointment surged through her like a wave, drowning her, strangling her. She struggled to catch her breath. Her heart raced and she fought off panic. She couldn't go through that again. She wouldn't. And if Del had done it to Camille, he could do it to her.

She gave Camille a weak smile. "Well, it was

nice chatting with you." That sounded so stupid, even to her ears. Nice chatting with her? How about thanks for blowing up my world? That would have been more truthful.

Camille bobbed her head, her curls bouncing in perfect timing on her shoulders. "Yes, nice chatting. We women need to stick together against scoundrel men, don't we?"

Cassandra grabbed her purse and fled the ladies' room, her heart pounding. She looked around the ballroom wildly and spotted Uncle Ted. She threaded her way through the crowd, bumping into people as she rushed. "Excuse me. Sorry."

She finally reached her uncle. "I'm feeling a bit under the weather. I'm going to head up to my room."

"Are you okay?" He frowned and looked at her closely.

"I'm fine. Just... tired."

"I'll call and check on you tomorrow."

"Okay. Good night, Uncle Ted. Night, Patricia." And with that she fled the ballroom and up the grand stairway, her hand trailing on the polished wood railing. She cut over to the stairs at the end of the hallway, hoping to avoid seeing anyone. She quickly climbed to the top floor to her suite, out of breath.

As she entered the room, hot tears trailed down her cheeks. She quickly closed the door behind her. Kicking off her shoes, she dropped her purse on the table and walked over to open the balcony doors. Stepping outside into the cool air, she let it rush around her, soothe her.

Only there was no soothing to be had.

Her world tilted out of balance. Everything she'd been so happy about just hours before disintegrated in the cool night air that taunted her damp cheeks.

Delbert had cheated on his long-term girlfriend. Just like Vincent had cheated on her. Camille was right, the woman was always the last to know.

Well, she'd been warned now and she wasn't about to let it happen to her again. Ever. Her heart couldn't take it again. It was already crumbling into tiny shards of glass.

She stared out at the sea, so familiar, and yet so… empty. Lonely. Cold.

Her mind played cruel tricks on her as she pictured Del slipping away to a quiet corner with that woman in the black gown. She gulped in a breath of the salty air, trying to chase away the image. No, she couldn't go through being cheated on again.

With that, she made up her mind. She'd head back home tomorrow.

CHAPTER 21

D el searched the ballroom for Cassandra. It had taken longer than he hoped with Mrs. VanBuren. But she'd wanted to talk to him about having her daughter's wedding at the hotel. Not something he normally dealt with personally, but Evelyn was busy and the hotel's wedding planner wasn't here tonight. Not to mention Mrs. VanBuren had given a sizable donation to the history museum tonight.

He'd felt it was his responsibility to at least show her around and talk to her, and wow, could the woman talk. He finally gave her the wedding planner's business card and excused himself. But it had taken way more time than he'd wanted. Now all he wanted was to find Cassandra and go somewhere quiet. Away from the crowds. Steal a kiss or two. A smile slipped across his lips at the thought.

He spied Ted and Patricia across the room and headed that way, stopping too many times to smile and say hello to people. He finally reached the other side of the room.

"Ted, I'm looking for Cassandra. Have you seen her?"

"She wasn't feeling well and headed up to her room. I think she looked a bit pale." Ted's forehead creased. "And she said she was tired."

"We've had some late nights. I guess they finally caught up with her." Regret swept through him, but he did his best to hide his disappointment. He'd hoped to have a few quiet moments with her as the event wound down. Maybe a nightcap on the porch. But they had been keeping late hours. Not surprising that she'd be tired.

Camille came walking up to them, clinging to a man's arm. At closer inspection, he saw it was Charlie, Donna's ex-husband. Well, that was a change from the senator or the CEO of the bank.

"Camille." He nodded, wondering why she kept showing up here at the hotel. Was there no other place in Florida for her to hang out? "And Charlie, right?"

"Yes, that's Charlie." Patricia frowned at the couple. "What are you doing here?"

"Got as much right to be here as you and your—" Charlie grinned a menacing grin. "What do we call old Ted here, anyway? Your *boyfriend*? Ex-lover?"

"I think that's quite enough." Ted's voice was stern, cold, and brittle as ice.

"Ah, don't mind me. Patricia and I go way back. Though, I guess you go way back with Ted here, too." Charlie winked.

Delbert looked from Charlie to Camille. Looks like two troublemakers had found each other. Just great.

"I saw Cassandra tonight." Camille interrupted the exchange between Charlie and Patricia, flashing a smile that showed her perfect white teeth and flipping her curls behind her shoulder. "She looked lovely. She said she'd come here with you? So you two are dating?"

He didn't really want to answer her. He just dipped his chin briefly.

"Good luck with that," Cassandra said, eyeing him closely, a small smile on her lips.

He frowned. What did she mean by that?

"Though she doesn't live here, so I assume not much will come of it." Camille turned to Charlie. "I see the senator over across the room. Do you mind if we go over and say hi to him?"

Ah, now there was the Camille he knew. Always searching for someone better or more important to talk to.

"Of course we can, darlin'." Charlie turned to Ted and Patricia. "Great to see you again, Patty."

Patricia's mouth dropped open, but she quickly recovered her poise and nodded aloofly at him.

Camille and Charlie headed across the floor.

"I just detest that man," Patricia drilled out the words as she watched Charlie leave.

"Don't let him upset you." Ted put his arm around Patricia's shoulder.

"He always was one to cause trouble. I wish he'd decide it was time to leave town." She shrugged. "He rarely stays this long, and I'm sure once he leaves it will be years before we see him again. Good riddance."

"Well, I should go mingle some more. Make the rounds," Del said as he watched the crowd swallow Charlie and Camille. He kind of felt like Patricia. Good riddance. "You two have a good evening."

He headed out into the crowd, but in the opposite direction of Charlie and Camille. Smiling and making small talk to the guests no longer had much appeal. Maybe he'd sneak off and head to his suite. The night sure hadn't ended like he'd hoped it would. He'd really wanted to have some time alone with Cassandra. He would call her first thing tomorrow and check on her. And he made himself a promise not to keep her out so late night after night.

CHAPTER 22

Cassandra packed her bag the next morning, carefully folding up her beautiful new gown. Not that she'd ever wear it again. It would just remind her of last night. And she wanted nothing that would bring back the memory. How magical the night had been at first, then the devastation that enveloped her when Camille told her about Delbert's infidelities. She closed her eyes tightly for a moment and sucked in a deep breath.

She closed the suitcase and slid it to the floor. Turning slowly, she glanced over at the balcony doors. She couldn't help herself. She needed one last look from the balcony, from her favorite suite at the hotel, because she never planned to return here again.

She stepped out on the balcony, and sadness overwhelmed her. The thought of not returning to her beloved hotel brought as much pain as knowing that she and Delbert were finished.

The fresh breeze flowed around her, ruffling the fabric of her dress. A pair of sailboats sliced through the water. Two gulls flew overhead, calling to each other, oblivious of her. The world just kept going on around her, while emptiness hammered down on her.

She closed her eyes, searing the view, the memory, deep into her mind, then headed inside. Feeling lost—which she shouldn't be feeling because the room was so familiar—she swept her gaze around the room, taking in every tiny detail.

She panicked slightly at the sound of a knock at the door. She wasn't ready to face Delbert, if that was him. If she saw Del, she wanted it to be on her terms, and certainly not here in her suite.

She took a deep breath and peered through the peephole.

Thank goodness. Uncle Ted.

She opened the door. "Come in. I was just going to come and see you."

Ted glanced over at her suitcase. "Are you leaving?"

"I am. Business calls."

He looked at her closely, unconvinced. "You sure that's all it is?"

"That's all." She forced a smile but knew it was a weak one.

"You'd tell me if something was wrong, wouldn't you?"

She closed her eyes for a moment. "It's just... time for me to go."

"Something happened, didn't it?"

"I don't really want to talk about it. I just... I need to go."

Ted wrapped her in his strong arms. "I'm here for you. You know that."

"I know." She hugged him back, then stepped out of his embrace.

"Will you come back soon?"

"I'm not sure when it will be. Work is picking up." She avoided his gaze.

He looked at her closely for a long moment, then kissed her lightly on the cheek. "I'm always here. Always."

She nodded, fighting back tears as she saw him to the door.

"I love you, Cassie." He sent her a worried look as he walked out.

"I love you, too." She closed the door behind him. Only one more thing to do before she left. She'd avoided it as long as she could, but it had to be done. On her terms. She grabbed her suitcase and headed down to the lobby, hardening her heart with every step.

She paused outside of Del's office and drew in a deep breath as she knocked.

"Come in."

She turned the cold metal doorknob and stepped inside. Delbert's face broke into a warm smile. "Cassie. There you are. Are you feeling okay? Ted said you were tired and went up to your suite early last night."

"I'm fine." She remained in the open doorway. "I need a moment to talk to you."

"Of course."

She took one tiny step inside, and Delbert frowned when he saw her suitcase.

"What's this? Are you leaving?"

"I am. I need to get back to work."

"But, so suddenly?" Delbert got up and walked over to her. "I feel like you just got here. We've just found each other again."

She backed up a step. "I know. But really, it's

kind of silly to start something up, isn't it? I have a job across the country. You live here."

"I don't feel like we're just starting something up. I feel like it's been going on for a very long time." He looked at her closely, and she had to keep herself from backing up all the way into the hallway from the intensity of his gaze.

She steeled herself against his pleading look, remembering Camille's words.

"I guess our timing is just destined to be wrong." Very wrong. Because there was no way she was going to date a man who cheated. She could ask him about what Camille had told her, but Del would deny it, just like Vincent had tried to deny his cheating.

He reached out and touched her hand, scorching her, but she willed the feeling away, demanding she only feel an icy cold.

"I'm sorry. But I've really thought this over, and it just won't work out between us." She stared down at where he was still touching her and slowly moved her hand away.

"I don't understand. This is so sudden. Stay awhile. Let's talk through this. I know we can figure this out." His tone was insistent, bordering on pleading.

"I have thought this through. It's just too… complicated." She reached for her suitcase. "I need to go. I have a ride waiting to take me to the airport."

"I could drive you. It will give us time to talk." He looked at her intently.

"No, I've already called a ride."

"Cassie—"

"Goodbye, Del. Please don't make this any harder than it is. Please. I just need to go home. Let me go. It's for the best. It's what I need." She took one last long look at him. The man she loved. The man who in time she was going to learn not to love. Not to care a thing about. The friend from her past. The man who she'd just found again. All that would be buried deep inside, far away from any memory.

She turned to leave.

"Cassie… I love you. I always will. Nothing will change that." His words swirled around her, teased her, tormented her.

She paused for a moment, fighting back tears, then continued to walk away. Down the hall and out into the familiar lobby. Walking through The Cabot for the last time. Determined never to return.

"Cassie, wait."

She turned to see Ted hurrying up to her, a cup of coffee in his hand, a frown on his face. "I decided to grab some coffee after I was up talking to you and I saw you across the lobby. I can tell something is wrong. What is it?"

"Oh, Uncle Ted." She crumbled into his arms, and he held her tight. "I'm just... sad. Things didn't work out with Del and me." Her voice cracked. "I need some time and distance."

"What did he do?" Ted pulled away and searched her face.

"Nothing," she whispered. "It isn't... wasn't..." She dashed away her tears and cleared her throat. "I'll be fine. I just need to go home. Work. Keep busy." She kissed her uncle. "I have to go. A car is waiting for me. I'll call you soon." She turned and fled out of the lobby into the blinding sunshine. The sunshine that mocked her mood, her anger, her hurt. The sky flooded down sunbeams and cheerful bird songs when what she wanted was a raging, thunderous storm that only Florida could produce. One to match her tempestuous mood.

Del sat back down at his desk, stunned. The air in his office stifled him, suffocated him. How did he and Cassandra get from I love you to it won't work? And how had it happened so suddenly? Why wouldn't she at least talk to him? Part of him wanted to go running after her. But she'd asked him not to make it harder on her. And he'd do anything to make things easier for her. Anything. Even let his own heart shatter into tiny pieces.

He lowered his head into his hands as loneliness and despair washed over him. Now what? Maybe if he gave her some time, they could talk. Work things out. Distance wasn't a reason to not see each other. Not if they loved each other. And he did love her. Truly and deeply, a feeling more overwhelming than any emotion he'd ever felt.

He jumped to his feet. He had to go after her. Had to.

The door to his office flew open. "What did you do?" Ted Cabot's thunderous words echoed across the room as he stood there, a furious expression on his face. "I told you not to hurt her, son. I don't know what you did, but she was very upset."

"That's just it." He shook his head as

despair swept over him again. "I don't know what I did, either. She said we have very different lives in different places. But that was all so sudden. Just the day before... well, I love your niece and I told her that. I've loved her almost my whole life. It just took me a while to find her again and tell her."

"Well, something happened. She looked heartbroken."

"I should go after her." He stepped around Ted.

Ted caught his arm. "No, you leave her be. I don't know what happened, but I do know she wants to go home. She's made this decision, and you abide by it. Don't you hurt her any more than you already did."

"I just don't know what happened." He closed his eyes to the pain searing through him before turning to stare at Ted. "I honestly don't know."

"I won't have you hurting her. I warned you. So now you stay away from her, do you hear me?" Ted jabbed his finger against Del's chest.

Del swallowed, not answering. How could he possibly promise to stay away from her?

"If this is what she needs, to be far away from you, then you give that to her." Ted looked directly at him. "If what you said is true… that you love her… then you give her what she asked for. Distance."

Ted spun around and walked out the door.

Del crossed over and sat on the edge of his desk, his mind a whirl of thoughts, his emotions churning through him.

Was Ted right? Should he let Cassandra have what she asked for? Should he just let her go? He *did* love her, and that was what she'd asked of him.

He let out a long sigh. At the very least, he should give her some time. Maybe after they were apart for a while, she'd miss him. Maybe when she thought about it more, she'd return. Maybe she'd be willing to try again.

Maybe.

He clung to that hope.

CHAPTER 23

Austin drove along Poinciana Drive, thinking that it would eventually lead to a road that connected to Gulf Avenue and his cottage. After staying at Livy's for a few days, he needed to go grab some more things from his house. Why did he never remember that Moonbeam was a tangled mess of streets and canals, and even if you were close to an area, often you couldn't quite get there because of a canal cutting off access so that you needed to take the long way around? Poinciana dead-ended into a canal. He turned his car around in frustration. Then he frowned as the car sputtered and he barely made it to the edge of the road before it jerked to a complete stop.

He frowned. What the heck was going on?

He glanced at the gas gauge in disbelief. Empty. He never ran out of gas. Never. He was too organized for that. He guessed he'd been too occupied with the wedding last week and being newly married, living at Livy's, and out of his normal routine. He leaned his head on the steering wheel and let out a long, drawn-out sigh.

A man walked up to the side of the car and tapped on the window. Austin rolled down the window as the man nodded toward the hood of the car. "Car problems?"

"Ran out of gas," he said sheepishly.

"Happens." The man nodded again. "I've got some in the garage. Let me get some for you." The man stretched out his hand. "Josh Tyler."

"Austin Woods. I appreciate your help." He climbed out of the car and followed Mr. Tyler toward the house and up onto a long porch. A sign leaned against the railing with large red letters. For Sale.

He looked up at the house as a shiver ran through him. "Mr. Tyler?"

"Hm?" The man paused.

"Are you putting your house on the market?" He tilted his head toward the sign.

"I am. The missus and I are moving up to Jacksonville. Our daughter and grandkids live up there and my wife misses them." He grinned and shrugged. "I'd do anything to keep the missus happy."

"My wife and I are looking for a new house. We recently got married. I wonder... would you mind showing me your house?"

"Not at all. Come on in." The man led him into the house. "Mary, we have company. Austin here is looking for a house for him and his bride."

"And Livy's daughter. Emily."

"Oh, you married one of the Parker women, did you? The one who runs the Parker Cafe."

And while he knew to never call it *Parker* Cafe, he figured now wasn't the time to correct the woman that it was really Sea Glass Cafe. So he just nodded. "I did."

"That's wonderful. Those Parker women are good people." Mary bobbed her head vigorously. "So, you're looking for a new place to live?"

"I am."

"Well, come on. Let me show you around. Don't mind all the boxes. We were trying to get some of our things packed up before putting the

KAY CORRELL

house on the market. Josh says we're packing up the junk, but I say it's all things that are needed."

Mary led him through the kitchen with its nice, updated appliances. Then they walked through the living room and she threw open the French doors to reveal a long covered porch overlooking the bay. "Wow, the view is great."

"I will miss this view. But not as much as I miss seeing my grandkids all the time." She turned. "Come. I'll show you upstairs."

The upstairs had a huge master bedroom and a bath with a big clawfoot tub as well as a walk-in shower.

"There are two walk-in closets, too. That was Josh's idea when we remodeled the upstairs. It used to be four tiny bedrooms. We made it into a bigger master bedroom and bath, and then one of the other bedrooms—the one that overlooks the canal—that's larger now, too."

Josh told him what they were hoping to get for the house, and Austin was thrilled that it was a fair price.

He walked over and looked at the view from the master bedroom. Doors opened out onto a second-floor balcony large enough for a small table and two chairs. He could imagine having morning coffee with Livy out there. He turned to the Tylers. "Your house is just... great. So great. It would be *perfect* for us."

Mary broke into a wide grin. "That's good to hear. Why don't you go get your wife and her daughter and bring them over to see the house?"

"You know what? I will. I think they're both at the cafe now, but I'll go find them." Excitement rushed through him. The house was perfect. Right on the harbor, but a canal ran up the side. They could dock Livy's boat there and she could still boat to see Donna or take it out on the harbor.

They went back downstairs, and he headed for the door. "I'll be back soon."

"Aren't you forgetting something?" Josh asked.

He frowned. "What?"

"The gas." Josh grinned.

"Oh, right." Austin shook his head and laughed. "I'll need that."

Livy looked up from where she was scrubbing the ice cream counter to a polished finish to see Austin rushing up to her, his cheeks flushed.

"There you are." Austin pressed a quick kiss to her cheek. "Where's Emily?"

"She's in the kitchen with Evelyn."

"Do you think you two could get away for an hour or so?"

She looked at him closely. "Probably. It's after the lunch rush and Melody's here, too."

"Perfect. I've got a surprise for you both."

"What is it?"

"If I told you, it wouldn't be a surprise, now would it?" He grinned at her.

She went and got Emily and they got into Austin's car. Emily grilled Austin with questions about where they were going but had no better luck than she had.

He didn't drive far before he turned down Poinciana Drive. "Where are you going? This is a dead-end. Runs into Dolphin Canal."

"I know that now." He grinned at her as he stopped in front of a well-kept Victorian house at the end of the street.

They got out of the car and stood in front of the house. "It's for sale," Austin explained. "I went in and saw it earlier. I think you're both going to love it."

"For real. Right here on Dolphin Canal and the harbor?" Emily's eyes widened.

"How did you find it?" Livy asked.

"Would you believe I ran out of gas right in front of it? The owner came out to offer help, and I found out they're getting ready to put it on the market." He grabbed her hand. "Come on, the Tylers are expecting us."

She climbed the steps to the front porch lined with hibiscus and gardenia bushes. A large Poinciana tree shaded the porch.

The door swung open and an older couple stood in the doorway, smiling. She recognized them from coming into Parker's over the years.

"I'm Mary, and this is Joshua. Come in."

They walked inside, and Livy grabbed Austin's arm. "Oh, Austin."

The room was large and airy and reached all the way to the back of the house. Mary showed them around, and with each room, Livy's excitement grew. The house would be perfect for them.

They headed upstairs, and she almost gasped at the large bedroom and beautiful view of the bay.

"And look, two closets." Austin grinned. "I hope to get at least half of one."

She laughed. "We could work with that."

Emily came walking out of the large bedroom overlooking the canal. "That bedroom is sweet. Twice the size of the one I have now. And did you see the hall bathroom? It's huge."

"So do you two like the house?" Austin asked.

"Love it," Emily said.

"I think it's perfect." She hugged Austin.

"So, you want to buy it?" Mary looked at each of them. "I'd love to have you all living here. I was worried about who we'd sell it to. Worried that they might not appreciate it. Or maybe they were buying it for rental property. I want someone to buy it who will love it as much as we do."

"That would be us," Livy assured her. "We'll love it."

They all walked downstairs. "So, we can get all this sale sorted out legally if you're sure you want it," Josh said as they stood in the large family room.

Austin looked at her, and she nodded, a wide grin spreading across her face.

Austin shook hands with Josh. "Sounds like we've got a deal."

They walked outside and said goodbye to the Tylers. Livy paused, her hand on Austin's arm. "So… this thing you and your mother have about running out of gas… it seems to work out quite well for you."

Austin grinned. "It does, doesn't it? Guess we're just lucky like that."

"I'm glad you found it. It will be the perfect place for all of us." She stood on tiptoe and kissed his cheek.

"Hey, are you two going to just stand there kissing all day, or can we go?" Emily stood by the car, grinning at them. "We've got a lot of packing to do, you know."

Austin took her hand. "Em's right. We've got a lot to do."

"And I can't wait to move in." She took one more look at the house as they headed down the walkway to the street. Soon, this would be their house, their yard, their street. Her heart hummed with happiness, and she squeezed Austin's hand.

CHAPTER 24

Patricia didn't know how time had a way of slipping by so quickly these days. It had already been a few weeks—almost a month—since Livy's wedding. Poor Cassandra had been gone three weeks or so, and Ted was really worried about her. Time seemed to rush by now, and she wasn't sure she was entirely comfortable with that, not that she could do anything about it. The days and hours seemed a bit more precious these days.

She shook her head and got ready to go to Ted's apartment for dinner. They ate dinner together almost every day now, either down in the dining room at Sunrise, or out at a restaurant, or, like tonight, Ted would cook for her at his apartment. The man loved to cook and was very skilled at it. And she had to admit, it was nice to just spend time alone with him.

She dressed in black slacks and a pale blue top, then stood in the closet staring at her huge selection of shoes. Just a few months ago, she would have reached for some high heels, but now she grabbed a pair of simple, black flats. How things had changed since she'd started dating Ted. The ever so stylish, but so uncomfortable, shoes were relegated to the back of her closet and rarely worn.

At the last moment, she decided to add her favorite string of pearls. As far as she was concerned, it was never wrong to add pearls.

At precisely six o'clock, she headed to Ted's suite.

He opened the door, dressed in nice slacks and a button-down shirt with the cuffs rolled up to almost his elbows. The man always looked so impossibly handsome.

"You going to stand there staring at me, or come in?" His lips twitched as he held back a grin.

"I wasn't staring I was just—" She stepped inside and shook her head. A grown woman, staring rapturously at her date. What had she turned into?

He kissed her quickly on the cheek. "You were staring, though." He laughed as he walked into the suite.

He'd set the table with nice dishes, candles, and flowers. Ted never did anything halfway, that was for sure. "The table looks lovely."

He beamed at her. "Thank you. I thought we'd have a fancy meal tonight. Been cooking and baking all day. Why don't you sit and I'll get you a drink?"

"It smells wonderful." She sank gracefully onto the couch.

He handed her a drink and settled beside her. "I have about thirty minutes before I need to finish up the last-minute things in the kitchen."

He knew just how long she liked to sip on a glass of wine before a meal, too. He knew so many little details about her. She liked that about him. Liked it a lot. It made her feel special and cared about. It was comfortable being with him, and they could talk for hours about everything and nothing. He accepted her as she was, even when she was in one of her prickly moods—which she knew she got into. But things that used to seem so important to her, like designer shoes and town gossip, just didn't matter as much. She had changed since finding Ted again, and she admitted she liked this new version of herself. Who knew she could change after all this time?

She turned to concentrate on what he was saying and they chatted about their day until Ted got up to set their meal on the table. He'd outdone himself this time. Everything was delicious.

After dinner, he cleared the table and insisted she go back to sit on the couch. When he finished, he came to sit beside her and took her hand. She liked how he did that now. Just took her hand as if it belonged in his.

He looked at her intently, though, and it threw her off guard.

"Patricia, I wanted to talk to you."

Such a serious expression on his face. She frowned slightly. "Of course."

"We've been dating for a while now—"

"Not that long," she interrupted him, wondering how long it had been. It seemed like it had only been an instant, but then it also felt like they'd been dating forever. Time playing tricks again.

He took her other hand in his. "I love you, Patricia. I have since I met you all those years ago. And now that we've found each other again… well… I wondered…"

This was not like Ted. He was always so cool and collected.

"I wanted to ask you…"

All of a sudden, her heart started pounding, and her pulse raced. She stared at him, waiting for him to continue.

"Would you marry me, Patricia? I'd like nothing more than to become your husband. To spend all my time with you."

She tried to concentrate on his words. Marry him. Ted. After all these years. To be married to someone who loved her. But they were so… Well, they weren't very young anymore. Wasn't it silly to get married at this stage of life?

He sat there patiently, knowing that she had to sort out her thoughts. He knew her so well. When to push, when to hold back.

"I… don't know what to say," she finally managed to murmur.

"Say you'll marry me." He flashed her a disarming smile.

"But—" Then all of a sudden she couldn't think of one reason *not* to marry Ted. She loved him. She had forever. She'd just never thought she'd actually have this with him. A life together with him. And suddenly she knew that's what she wanted. Truly and deeply wanted.

"So?" He cocked his head, watching her face.

"Yes. Yes, I'll marry you, Ted Cabot." She knew she must look ridiculous with a dopey grin on her face but didn't care one bit.

"Yes!" He jumped to his feet, hurried over to the bookcase, and returned with a small box. He popped it open and showed it to her. A beautiful diamond ring. And she loved it, of course, because it seemed like Ted knew her better than she knew herself.

"It's lovely, Ted."

He slipped it onto her finger, and it fit perfectly. She glanced down at it as it sparkled in the lamplight. He sat beside her again and wrapped his arm around her shoulder. "You've made me a very happy man."

She looked right into his eyes. "And you make me very happy, too. I can't wait to marry you."

"Great. Then there's no reason to wait, is there?"

"There isn't." Hadn't she just been thinking about how quickly time passed?

"So we'll tell your family when we go to Donna's tomorrow for the barbecue?"

"Yes, we'll tell them then." And pick a date. Because time was fragile and she didn't want to waste any of it. She wanted to spend the rest of her days with Ted.

CHAPTER 25

Donna liked nothing better than a nice, big family gathering on a Sunday afternoon. She didn't work at Parker's on Sundays, though she often popped in to check on things. Melody had taken over running the cafe on Sundays, so Livy and Evelyn had Sundays off, too.

Barry was busy barbecuing up burgers and brats as everyone started arriving. Livy, Emily, and Austin came in, chattering about the new house they were moving to next week. Heather, Jesse, and Blake arrived with a large salad and chilled champagne and orange juice for mimosas. Evelyn and Rob came with two of Evelyn's pies. Finally, Ted and Patricia walked out on the lanai.

Ah, her whole family was here, just like she liked it. She caught Barry smiling at her, sensing her contentment, and smiled back at him.

Her mother looked unusually pretty tonight. Her cheeks were flushed, and she held hands with Ted as they walked around saying hi to everyone. She couldn't be more pleased that her mother was dating Ted. They seemed to make each other very happy, and her mother sure had mellowed in the last few months.

Evelyn walked over and nodded toward Patricia and Ted. "Mom looks good, doesn't she?"

"I was just thinking that. I think Ted is good for her," she said as Heather and Jesse passed around champagne, beer, and soda.

Ted walked over to the edge of the lanai and tapped a knife against his beer bottle. "Excuse me."

Everyone turned to look at him, and Patricia moved over to stand by his side.

"I have a bit of an announcement to make. I've asked Patricia to marry me."

Donna gasped and stared at them.

"And I said yes." Patricia held up her hand and flashed a large diamond ring.

"And I couldn't be happier." Ted grinned.

Evelyn raised her glass. "To Mother and Ted and a life of happiness together."

"To Patricia and Ted," everyone chimed in.

Donna rushed over and hugged her mother and Ted. "This is great news."

"We're pretty happy about it." Ted still wore a lopsided grin.

"And we want to get married right away," Patricia added.

"You do?" Heather and Jesse walked up to them.

"We do. We just need to decide where."

"The Cabot?" Donna suggested. Their ballroom seemed like a fitting place for her mother's wedding. Fancy, elegant.

"Ah… I don't think The Cabot will work. Cassandra is coming, and there is that whole mess with her and Delbert," Patricia pointed out. Donna was stunned at her mother's unusual sensitivity to Cassandra's situation.

"You're welcome to have it on The Destiny," Jesse offered.

Patricia's brows drew together slightly, then her lips slipped into a smile. "You know what? I think that would be a nice idea. Your and Heather's wedding was lovely."

Donna raised her eyebrows. Her mother was

going to get married on a boat? She glanced over at Evelyn, who grinned and shrugged.

"I think The Destiny is a fabulous idea." Ted nodded.

"There, it's all decided, then," Heather said. "Jesse, go check your schedule and see if you can make it happen."

Jesse pulled out his phone while they all watched him. "If you want a weekend, like a Saturday or Sunday, it will be like three months out." He looked up from his phone.

"I'm not waiting that long." Patricia insisted. "How about a Friday?"

"I have one in four weeks." Jesse looked up and grinned.

"Perfect. Then that will be our wedding day."

"We'll help with everything," Livy offered. "We're getting kind of good at these quick weddings."

Donna laughed. "We are. It's almost getting to be a Parker tradition."

"I'm sure you girls will help me make the day perfect," Patricia said, then beamed a smile at Ted.

Donna just stared at her mother. Yes, her

mother sure had changed since Ted had come back into her life. Happier. More relaxed. And definitely in love.

CHAPTER 26

D el sat out on the porch of the owner's
suite, sipping a drink and staring off into
the distance, not really seeing anything. He'd
grabbed his phone like a million times to call
Cassandra in the weeks since she left. But Ted's
words hung over him. "Give her what she
wants. Give her space."

But all the joy had been sucked out of his
world now. He threw himself into work,
finishing up everything on his always-too-long
to-do list. He'd researched new properties for
the Hamilton Hotel chain to acquire. He'd
organized his office at the hotel and here in the
owner's suite. He'd even cleaned out the
thousands of old emails on his computer. But

nothing kept him busy enough because he was still here at the hotel, tormented by memories.

The Cabot Hotel that had brought him such joy not too long ago was now a painful place to walk through. So many memories. So many what-ifs. The what-ifs were strangling him.

He finally made a pact with himself. He'd give Cassandra another month to work through whatever she thought were their problems. Then he was going to fly out and see her. Track her down. Talk to her.

He'd come up with a million ways they could be together. He'd give up living at The Cabot and move near her. Or, if she wanted, she could work remotely at The Cabot and fly back home when she needed to for business. He'd live on the moon if he could just be with her.

He still didn't know why all of a sudden she'd gotten cold feet. Decided to leave without discussing it with him. It wasn't like her. They'd grown so close, talked about everything.

Ted had said that Cassandra had a hard time trusting men. But he'd done nothing to break her trust. He never would.

He stared up as a lone blue heron flapped rhythmically by in the sky. "You lonely, too?" He come visit, but she wasn't ready for Moonbeam. She didn't know if she'd ever be.

Tonight she'd come home a bit earlier than normal because exhaustion had just about brought her to her knees. She sat at the table, picking at some takeout she'd grabbed on the way home.

Her phone rang, and she glanced at it. Uncle Ted. She debated letting it go to voicemail, not sure she was up to playing twenty questions with him again.

Yes, I'm fine.

No, don't worry about me.

Not sure when I'm coming back to Moonbeam.

But she sighed and answered the phone. "Hi."

"Cassandra, great. Glad I reached you. I have news." It was hard not to recognize the excitement in Ted's voice.

"What news?"

"So—and I hope you'll be happy about this —I asked Patricia to marry me. She said yes."

"Oh, I'm so happy for you. That's wonderful news." And she was happy for him. He deserved this. And Patricia made him very happy.

"And one other bit of news."

sent his words skyward, but the bird didn't answer. It just continued to fly away, leaving him… just like Cassandra had.

He let out a long sigh. Sitting around bemoaning his fate wasn't helping anything. Maybe he'd take an extended business trip. Take four or five weeks to check on Hamilton Hotel properties. That would keep him busy… and keep him away from The Cabot and the way the hotel haunted him now.

CHAPTER 27

Cassandra worked long, hard hou
coming home late at night so she cou
just drop exhausted into bed. Though sle
eluded her most nights until the early hours
the morning.

But no matter how long or hard she worke
the pain still grabbed her and sucked her brea
away. Wasn't it supposed to get better as tir
went by? It had only been about a month, but
far, the pain hadn't lessened.

Maybe because she'd already been here wi
Vincent. Learning that she didn't really kno
the man as well as she thought she did.

Ted called her a couple of times a wee
checking on her. The last time he'd asked her

She waited for him to tell her. Something bigger than him getting married?

"We're getting married in four weeks."

"You're what?"

"We decided that we've been apart long enough. There's no use wasting any of our days. We're getting married on The Destiny, Jesse Brown's boat. That's surprising, right? But that's what we decided."

"That's great."

"So, you'll come?"

"Of course, I will." But she really, really didn't want to go back to Moonbeam. And where would she stay? There was no way she was staying at The Cabot.

"Good. I was hoping you wouldn't stay away because of—" He paused for a long moment before continuing. "I'm just glad you're coming."

"I'll be there. I promise."

"And Violet said she has a cottage for you if you want it." Ted paused. "I didn't think you'd want to stay at The Cabot."

"Thank you. I'd love to stay at the Blue Heron. I'll call tomorrow and reserve a cottage." At least that would work. Far away from The Cabot. And she was certain that Ted wouldn't invite Delbert. So, with any luck, she'd get into town and back out without even seeing him.

"Great. I'll talk to you soon. Can't wait to see you."

"Good night."

"Night, Cassie. Sleep well."

Sleep well. She only hoped her body and mind would listen to Uncle Ted's words. Worrying about a trip back to Moonbeam probably wasn't going to help...

CHAPTER 28

Patricia stood on the top level of The Destiny, dressed in a light blue suit. She was quite pleased with how it fit. She held a small bouquet of white roses and blue hydrangeas. Her favorite pearls nestled against her collarbone, and her hair was twisted up in a fancy knot that Donna had assured her looked lovely.

She had to keep from pinching herself because she couldn't really believe that more than fifty years after falling in love with Ted Cabot, she was marrying him. That he wanted to marry her. That he made her so happy.

And she *was* happy. A truly unfamiliar feeling for her.

"You ready, Mom?" Donna asked her, touching her arm.

"I am." She adjusted her suit jacket slightly, surprised at how nervous she was, even though she was one hundred percent sure about marrying Ted.

"There's the music starting." Evelyn leaned close.

She took a deep breath and drew her shoulders up, standing her full height. Donna stood on one side of her and Evelyn on the other as she stepped into the aisle, her pulse racing and her heart swelling with happiness.

Ted's face broke into a wide smile as she walked toward him, and her nervousness dissolved. "You look beautiful," he said to her as he took her hand. He held her hand through the short ceremony, only releasing it to slip a wedding band on her finger.

He kissed her at the end of the service, and her heart soared. Married. She was Mrs. Cabot now. Still holding hands, they walked back down the aisle together as the sky burst into brilliant colors of orange, yellow, and blue.

"Perfect timing. My first sunset with my wife," he whispered in her ear.

The radiant sunset matched her mood as

they headed down to the lower level of the boat for the reception, hand in hand, just like they were meant to be.

Cassandra stood against the expanse of windows at the reception. Patricia looked beautiful, and her uncle hadn't stopped grinning since the ceremony. They made the perfect couple. Finally, together after all those years apart.

Unlike her and Delbert.

That hadn't worked out for them. But she pushed the thought away. So far, she'd been lucky enough to not run into him since her return to Moonbeam. Not that she'd gone anywhere except her cottage at Violet's, a rehearsal dinner at Donna's place, and here on The Destiny. Pretty safe bet she wouldn't run into him at any of those places.

She had a flight tomorrow afternoon, which suited her just fine. Who knew when she'd come back to Moonbeam? She had no plans even though Ted wanted her to return soon. Maybe Ted and Patricia could come visit her.

Livy came walking up and handed her a

glass of champagne. "We should toast the happy couple. I can't believe the change in my grandmother. I think that maybe she just needed someone to really love her and not criticize her every move. Nelson, her first husband, was a mean, critical man. I think that's what finally hardened her into who she became."

"But look at her now. She looks so happy." She glanced over at the newlyweds.

"She does. And I'm very grateful that Ted makes her feel that way." Livy turned to her. "So, how are you?"

"I'm fine," she lied, wanting to avoid any deep conversations. She just wanted to make it through tonight and head home.

"I was just wondering—"

"Hey, Cassie. Come here for a minute." Ted waved from across the room.

Perfect. Escape.

She smiled ruefully at Livy, though honestly, she was glad to have an excuse to avoid talking to her. Because Livy had a way of keeping at it when she wanted to know something. And Cassandra was afraid that Livy wanted to know about her and Delbert. And that was one thing she didn't want to talk about. "I should go see what Ted wants. Thanks for the champagne."

She hurried off, feeling like she'd just escaped an inquisition.

CHAPTER 29

Cassandra packed the last of her things in her suitcase. She still had time before her ride came to get her to take her to the airport, but she was restless. She'd considered a walk on the beach but really thought the safest, Delbert-proof place to be was inside the cottage.

She heard a rap at the door. Probably Violet checking to see if she needed anything. The woman had done such a great job remodeling the cottages. The resort was lovely and welcoming. If she ever did decide to come to Moonbeam again... and she wasn't sure that would ever happen... she'd stay here at Blue Heron Cottages again.

She walked over and pulled open the door.

Livy stood there with two coffees. "Hi. I

didn't get to really talk to you last night, so I figured I'd bring you coffee this morning. Catch up with you before you leave."

She reached for the coffee. "Thank you." How was she going to escape Livy's questions this time?

"Come out and let's sit on the porch." Livy motioned to the cushioned chairs.

She glanced each direction, knowing it was silly to worry that Del would just suddenly pop up at the cottages, and walked outside.

They settled into the chairs, and Livy stretched out her legs before turning to look at her, her expression insincerely innocent. "So... how are you doing? I heard you and Del aren't seeing each other anymore. What happened?"

That didn't take her long. "It just didn't work out." She was going to leave it at that and see if she could dodge the subject.

Livy looked at her closely. "Why not?"

She sighed. Her newfound family wasn't much at leaving things alone when they wanted answers. "We live across the country from each other. We each have our jobs. Our homes in separate states."

"They've invented this thing called the airplane. You might have taken one here to come to the wedding." Livy rolled her eyes. "That's not it."

"You're not going to let this go, are you?" Though she knew Livy wasn't really prying. She was just concerned.

"Hey, Parker women never give up. So, what is it? What went wrong? Are you sure you can't work things out?"

Livy looked so hopeful, but there was no hope for her and Del. "I... there are just some things that I can't tolerate in a man."

Livy frowned. "I can't imagine what Del could ever do that you couldn't tolerate. He does work long hours... but so do you. It's not that, is it?"

She sighed, knowing that Livy wasn't going to drop it. And really, she kind of needed someone to talk to about it. She'd told no one. Not Ted. Nobody. "It's... I heard why Camille and Del broke up. She told me. He cheated on her. I just cannot go out with a cheater. Waiting for it to happen to me... again. Not after going through it with my ex-boyfriend."

Livy's eyes widened, and she set her cup down with a clatter. "That's not why they broke up. Not at all. And I can't imagine why she'd tell you that. Del is not the cheating type. And it's obvious that he's nuts about you." Livy's eyes narrowed. "Exactly what did Camille say?"

"She said that she found out Del cheated on her. With more than one person. And she was so surprised because she was the last to know." She shrugged. "Exactly like it was with Vincent. I never even had the slightest idea that he was cheating on me. Camille said we women need to stick together, so she told me so it wouldn't happen to me, too."

Livy's expression turned furious, and she reached over and grabbed her arm. "That's not what happened. Camille is... How should I say this? She's mean. Stuck up. Thinks she's better than everyone. She's... a liar."

Cassandra stared at Livy. Livy's impression of Camille did not jibe with hers. The woman had just tried to keep her from getting hurt by Del.

Livy shook her head. "You don't know her. The real Camille. She was mean to Emily when she was working on the history alcove at The Cabot. I think that was the last straw for Del because he was so proud of Emily and all the work she did. He called it quits with Camille. I think she thought he'd come back to her, but he didn't. So she showed up at the grand opening and acted like nothing had happened and they were still together. I guess she made a few choice remarks at the grand opening, and Delbert basically threw her out. Reiterated that they were no longer dating."

Cassandra frowned, trying to digest everything that Livy was saying. A quick memory flashed through her mind of Camille possessively grabbing Del's arm at the Grand Opening of the Cabot. A blunt remark Camille made about how the Cabots had let the hotel fall into disrepair.

"So, you see. Camille wasn't trying to do you a favor, woman to woman. She was trying to break up you and Delbert."

"So… Del broke up with her? Not the other way around?"

"Right." Livy nodded vigorously. "And really… you know Del. Can you actually imagine him cheating?"

"I didn't think Vincent, my ex-boyfriend, would cheat either. It's such a big button with me. I didn't think I'd ever learn to trust a man again after Vincent. But then I fell in love with Del… and then heard he cheated on Camille." Though she hadn't known Vincent as well as she knew Del. She'd known Del for years. Knew him so well…

She rubbed her arms as a cold wave of realization hit her.

No, there is no way that Del cheated on anyone. No way.

How could she have been so foolish?

Regret and embarrassment rushed through her. "Oh, Livy. What have I done? How could I have believed her? Why didn't I just talk to Del and tell him what Camille said? Let him explain. I should have talked to him."

"I guess you were scared. Frightened it would happen again like it did with your ex. But Del is different. He's kind."

"He's a wonderful man," she whispered. "And I've ruined everything."

"You haven't ruined everything," Livy grinned. "You know those romance movies where you want to scream at the actors to just go talk and it will all be sorted out? This is me screaming at you to go talk to Del. Head out right now to find him and tell him everything that happened. He'll understand."

"I don't know. I really hurt him. He might not trust me now." Panic swelled through her at the thought.

"You'll only know when you get a chance to see him. Go. Talk to him."

"I will. I'll try. Thank you for talking to me. Making me tell you what happened." She jumped up and hugged Livy.

"Hey, that's what family is for."

"I'm going to go find him right now."

Livy grinned. "Perfect. I'm sure you two can work it out."

"I hope so. I truly hope so."

CHAPTER 30

Del arrived back from a month-long business trip, checking on many of Hamilton Hotel's properties. It sure was better than sitting around The Cabot missing Cassandra. Hiding from the memories. Besides, it kept him busy until his self-imposed deadline. The day he'd fly out to see Cassie and talk to her after giving her time like she'd asked for. Well, she probably had asked for an indefinite time, but that just couldn't happen. He needed to talk to her. There was nothing the two of them couldn't work out. He was certain of that.

Almost certain.

He dropped his suitcase in the owner's suite and looked around. He could see Cassandra in every corner. Standing in the kitchen making dinner with him. Laughing on the couch. Talking out on the porch late into the night. He scrubbed his hands over his face. Maybe he wasn't quite ready to face being here at The Cabot after all. But an ice cream at Sea Glass cafe would make him feel better. The cafe's ice cream was always dependable. Always cheered him up. And, well, the cafe wasn't The Cabot.

He slipped out the door and headed to the cafe. The salty air pushed away his bad mood— or tried to—though the fact that Cassandra was gone was never far from his mind. He pushed from the sunshine into the cool air of the cafe, walked over to the ice cream counter, and sat on a stool. Livy walked out from the kitchen.

"Delbert, hi. Haven't seen you in a long time." She frowned as she looked at him.

"I was away on an extended business trip."

"Oh, really?"

"Just needed to…" He shrugged. "Get away."

"And you just got home?"

"Minutes ago. But your ice cream called to me."

Livy frowned again. "So I guess you might not have heard the news. Patricia and Ted got married yesterday."

"They did?" He jumped up. "Did Cassie come? Is she here in town?"

"She did, and she is. She's staying at The Blue Heron."

"I've got to go find her. Talk to her."

Livy looked over his shoulder, and her frown turned into a wide grin. "Oh, I don't think so."

"Why not? I have to find her."

"No, you don't. She's come to find you."

He whirled around at the sound of Cassandra's voice. "Cassie..." He wanted to reach out and touch her, make sure she was really there, but he held back.

"Del, I made a terrible mistake."

He held his breath. Had she changed her mind?

Please, say you've changed your mind.

Had he imagined her words?

"I... don't know if you'll be able to forgive me. I know I hurt you. And I'm sorry. I should have stayed and talked things out with you." She took a step closer. "I was just so... scared..."

"Scared of me?" His eyebrows rose.

"Yes. No. Let me explain. I was scared of getting hurt again."

"I'd never do anything to hurt you."

She pushed her curls away from her face.

"That night at the charity event for the history museum. You disappeared for quite a while."

"I know, I'm sorry—"

Cassie held up a hand to stop him. "I saw you across the room with this beautiful woman and I waved, but you didn't wave back."

He frowned. "I didn't see you wave. You mean when I was talking to Mrs. VanBuren? It was hotel business. A wedding she wanted to have there and Evelyn was so busy."

"No, that's okay. I believe you."

"But then, why did you leave?"

"I…" She looked him straight in the eye. "I ran into Camille in the ladies' room. And she told me that she broke up with you because you cheated on her. Multiple times."

"What?" Anger surged through him. "Cassie… I never…."

She held up a hand. "I know. Of course, you didn't. You're not that kind of man. I was so scared of getting hurt again after what Vincent did. I never suspected he was cheating on me. But you're not the same as Vincent. You're a better man. And I know you better. I know you deep into your soul. You are not a cheater. And I'm a fool. I can't believe I listened to Camille. And why didn't I just come straight to talk to you instead of running scared? Can you ever forgive me?"

He took two quick steps and gathered her into his arms. "Nothing to forgive. I'm just glad you're back." She fit exactly right in his arms, like she belonged there. Belonged there forever.

"I'm so sorry, Del. So sorry."

"I wish you would have come to talk to me. Promise me that if something ever comes up again, any problem, anything, that you'll talk to me."

"I promise."

He tilted her head up and settled a kiss on her lips. A kiss he'd been wanting to place there for weeks.

"So, you two just going to stand there in the middle of the cafe kissing, or do you want that ice cream you came in for?" Livy laughed.

Cassandra pulled out of his arms. "I do think this calls for a celebratory ice cream."

"I do, too." He kissed her again.

Suddenly, all the pieces of Cassandra's world fell into place. She was here with Delbert at her side. He'd forgiven her for her mistake. A hurtful, regrettable mistake. They would work through their problems—together—from now on. Her heart filled with happiness...

... and love. She loved this man so much. She slipped her hand in his as they sat at the counter.

Livy grinned at them. "Now you two lovebirds have to make a decision."

"You mean about where we'll live? How we'll work out the distance thing?" She frowned but knew that somehow she and Del would figure it out.

"No, actually, I was talking about what kind of ice cream you both want."

Del's delighted laugh rang out. "That's an easy decision. I'm having whatever she's having."

CHAPTER 31

D el walked into the lobby of The Cabot. He'd spent a glorious week with Cassie back here in Moonbeam. She'd just left to go take care of business but promised she'd be back within a week. And he was sure she would be. All was right with his world.

Then he looked across the lobby and spied Camille. Okay, not *everything* was right in his world. He strode across the distance, stopping right in front of her.

"Delbert, good evening."

"What are you doing here?"

"Not that it's any of your business, but I'm meeting Charlie for dinner."

He stood in front of her, blocking her way.

"You are no longer welcome at The Cabot." Camille gasped in surprise, but he didn't care. "I'd prefer if you never came to Moonbeam, but I know I can't control that. I *can* control who is welcome here at my hotel. I don't care who you're dating, or what the event is. You are not welcome. Do you understand?"

"You can't keep me out of The Cabot." Her eyes flashed in disbelief.

"Ah, but I can. You've worn out your welcome, do you understand? You've hurt the last person I care about, said the last mean thing, told the last lie."

"I—"

He held up a hand. "I don't want to hear it. You hurt people, Camille. And you don't ever seem to care. You say thoughtless, careless things. Or outright lies like you told Cassandra. That I cheated on you. *Why* would you say such a lie? I don't know why you do these things. But... you're not going to do them to people I care about. People I love."

"You think you love her?" Camille squeezed her designer clutch so hard he though she might damage it. That would probably be his fault, too.

"I *know* I love her."

260

"But… you've only known her for a little while. Just this year. We dated for years and you never told me that you loved me."

"Because I didn't. I never loved you. I simply… cared about you. I kept thinking you would change. But you'll never change, Camille. Never."

Her eyes darkened with anger. "You'll be sorry about this. Sorry that you're blocking me from your hotel. I know important people. I'll do everything I can to ruin you."

"Bring it, Camille. Just try."

"I will. And I'll win."

"Camille, none of this is about winning. It's about people. People with real feelings."

"I will ruin you and your company, Delbert Hamilton. If it's the last thing I do."

He shook his head. "It didn't have to be like this. We could have parted… if not friends, at least friendly acquaintances. But no. You just wouldn't let it go. I feel sorry for you, Camille. You have no real friends. You pop from boyfriend to boyfriend."

"Don't feel sorry for me. I have everything I want. Everything I need. Important men want to date me. They stand in line to date me."

"Ah, Camille." He shook his head. "But

none of that makes you happy, does it? I couldn't make you happy. They won't either. Only you can decide to be happy. Decide when you have enough. Decide… that people are more important than things or status or being invited to the next big event."

Camille sneered. "I wouldn't come back to any of your hotels if someone paid me to. I'll visit *nice* hotels from now on."

He shook his head. No, Camille would never change.

She glared at him, swirled around, and flounced away, her heels clicking on the tiled floor. She paused at the door and grabbed at Charlie's arm just as he was entering. She leaned in and talked animatedly for a moment. Charlie glanced back at him before taking her arm and ushering her out.

The man had no clue what he was in for with Camille…

But just like that, Camille Montgomery was out of his life forever. At least he hoped so. Poor Camille was never going to be a happy person. Never be content with her life. But that was no longer his problem. And he'd made it clear that she was no longer welcome at The Cabot, and he wouldn't stand for any of her interference in the lives of anyone he cared about.

"Goodbye, Camille," he whispered softly. "I hope that someday you find what you're looking for."

CHAPTER 32

The Parker women sat at Donna's kitchen table. Donna was pleased that her mother had started joining them frequently for the Official Parker Women Brunch, which they'd all decided was now the official name for their gathering.

"So, when Blake and I were leaving Parker's store last night, I touched the plaque beside the door that says established in 1926, just like you do, Grams. Blake asked me why you do that when you leave each night." Emily shrugged. "And I guess I've picked up the habit, too."

"Did you explain it to him?"

"I did. Said that it's your way of thanking Grace Parker for opening the store all those years ago."

"I am thankful Grace opened the store. And our family has so much history wrapped up in it. Just think, if Grace hadn't started Parker's General Store, so much would be different in our lives. We wouldn't have the store or the cafe. Who knows if we'd all be here in Moonbeam or not."

"Well, I'm glad we're here," Patricia said. "If I hadn't returned to Moonbeam, I'd never have met Ted again." She smiled, and it warmed Donna's heart to see her mother so happy.

"And I first met Barry at the store. The store has its own magic," Donna said as she thought of their first meeting and where it had led.

"And opening the cafe kept Heather around for longer than usual when she stayed to help us out." Evelyn draped an arm around Heather's shoulder and hugged her.

"And look where that led me. Married to Jesse and we have our son back." Heather smiled contentedly.

"I first met Rob at the ice cream counter." Evelyn looked pensive. "Maybe there is something magical about Parker's."

"I think there's a certain magic in being a Parker woman," Livy added, looking around the table at all of them, her eyes full of unquenchable love. "Look at us. Not everyone is lucky enough to have a family like ours."

"Just one of the many perks of being a Parker." Donna looked around at all of the Parker women gathered here in her kitchen. Just a simple get-together, but it filled her with such love, and she was so grateful for their strong bond.

"There are a lot of perks of being a Parker." Emily laughed. "Like unlimited free ice cream at Parker's Cafe."

"The Sea Glass Cafe," Livy and Heather said in unison, laughing.

A contented smile spread across Donna's face as she raised her glass. "To being a Parker woman, and the many perks that come with it."

They clinked glasses in a now-familiar toast to how blessed and lucky they all were and how grateful they were to be Parker women.

Dear Reader,

I hope you enjoyed the end of the Moonbeam Bay series. But don't worry, I can't leave these characters and places alone. My next series, Blue Heron Cottages, releases in June. (Yes, *those* cottages. The ones Violet bought and updated. So you'll see lots of your favorite Moonbeam characters again.) Preorder now so you don't miss it!

https://kaycorrell.com/blue-heron-cottages/

If you don't want to wait that long, you can try my standalone novel, Wind Chime Beach. Links to all retailers here:

https://kaycorrell.com/wind-chime-beach/

I want you to know how much I appreciate all my readers and I hope I give you a little bit of escape from real life. We all need that sometimes.

Happy reading,
Kay

ALSO BY KAY CORRELL

COMFORT CROSSING ~ THE SERIES

The Shop on Main - Book One

The Memory Box - Book Two

The Christmas Cottage - A Holiday Novella (Book 2.5)

The Letter - Book Three

The Christmas Scarf - A Holiday Novella (Book 3.5)

The Magnolia Cafe - Book Four

The Unexpected Wedding - Book Five

The Wedding in the Grove (crossover short story between series - Josephine and Paul from The Letter.)

LIGHTHOUSE POINT ~ THE SERIES

Wish Upon a Shell - Book One

Wedding on the Beach - Book Two

Love at the Lighthouse - Book Three

Cottage near the Point - Book Four

Return to the Island - Book Five

Bungalow by the Bay - Book Six

CHARMING INN ~ Return to Lighthouse Point

One Simple Wish - Book One

Two of a Kind - Book Two

Three Little Things - Book Three

Four Short Weeks - Book Four

Five Years or So - Book Five

Six Hours Away - Book Six

Charming Christmas - Book Seven

SWEET RIVER ~ THE SERIES

A Dream to Believe in - Book One

A Memory to Cherish - Book Two

A Song to Remember - Book Three

A Time to Forgive - Book Four

A Summer of Secrets - Book Five

A Moment in the Moonlight - Book Six

MOONBEAM BAY ~ THE SERIES

The Parker Women - Book One

The Parker Cafe - Book Two

A Heather Parker Original - Book Three

The Parker Family Secret - Book Four

Grace Parker's Peach Pie - Book Five

The Perks of Being a Parker - Book Six

BLUE HERON COTTAGES ~ THE SERIES

A six-book series coming in 2022.

WIND CHIME BEACH ~ A stand-alone novel

INDIGO BAY ~ Save by getting Kay's complete collection of stories previously published separately in the multi-author Indigo Bay series. The three stories are all interconnected.

Sweet Days by the Bay

Or buy them separately:

Sweet Sunrise - Book Three

Sweet Holiday Memories - A short holiday story

Sweet Starlight - Book Nine

ABOUT THE AUTHOR

Kay writes sweet, heartwarming stories that are a cross between women's fiction and contemporary romance. She is known for her charming small towns, quirky townsfolk, and enduring strong friendships between the women in her books.

Kay lives in the Midwest of the U.S. and can often be found out and about with her camera, taking a myriad of photographs which she likes to incorporate into her book covers. When not lost in her writing or photography, she can be found spending time with her ever-supportive husband, knitting, or playing with her puppies —two cavaliers and one naughty but adorable Australian shepherd. Kay and her husband also love to travel. When it comes to vacation time, she is torn between a nice trip to the beach or the mountains—but the mountains only get considered in the summer—she swears she's allergic to snow.

Learn more about Kay and her books at
kaycorrell.com

While you're there, sign up for her newsletter to hear about new releases, sales, and giveaways.

WHERE TO FIND ME:
kaycorrell.com
authorcontact@kaycorrell.com

Join my Facebook Reader Group. We have lots of fun and you'll hear about sales and new releases first!
www.facebook.com/groups/KayCorrell/

I love to hear from my readers. Feel free to contact me at authorcontact@kaycorrell.com

facebook.com/KayCorrellAuthor
instagram.com/kaycorrell
pinterest.com/kaycorrellauthor
amazon.com/author/kaycorrell
bookbub.com/authors/kay-correll